"There woman

Elizabeth gasped at Andrew's flat statement. "Of all the egotistical things to say . . . are you insinuating that I want to be in your life? As far as I'm concerned, you're just a man whom I met quite accidentally, and if it wasn't for the fact that I like your daughter very much, I wouldn't care if I never saw you again."

Andrew raised his eyebrows. "Your kisses say differently."

"So what? Can't a woman enjoy kissing as much as a man? I suppose your kisses mean that you want some kind of permanent attachment to me."

The look of horror on his face quickly answered her question. "Well," she went on, "marriage happens to be the last thing on my mind!"

Jeanne Allan lived in Nebraska, where she was born and raised, until her marriage to a United States Air Force lieutenant. More than a dozen moves have taken them to Germany and ten different states. Between moves, Jeanne spent time as a volunteer. With her two teenage children, she enjoys nature walks, bird-watching and photography at the family's cabin in the Colorado mountains, and she enjoys all kinds of crafts, including making stained-glass windows. She has always liked to write, but says her husband had to bully her into writing her first romance novel.

Jeanne Allan was named Romance Writer of the Year for 1989 by the Rocky Mountain Fiction Writers.

Books by Jeanne Allan

HARLEQUIN ROMANCE
2665—PETER'S SISTER
2845—WHEN LOVE FLIES BY
2875—THE WAITING HEART
2899—THE GAME IS LOVE
2935—TRUST IN LOVE
2989—ONE RECKLESS MOMENT
3073—BLUEBIRDS IN THE SPRING

Don't miss any of our special offers. Write to us at the following address for information on our newest releases.

Harlequin Reader Service
P.O. Box 1397, Buffalo, NY 14240
Canadian address: P.O. Box 603,
Fort Erie, Ont. L2A 5X3

NO ANGEL
Jeanne Allan

Harlequin Books

TORONTO • NEW YORK • LONDON
AMSTERDAM • PARIS • SYDNEY • HAMBURG
STOCKHOLM • ATHENS • TOKYO • MILAN

Original hardcover edition published in 1990
by Mills & Boon Limited

ISBN 0-373-03121-1

Harlequin Romance first edition May 1991

NO ANGEL

CHAPTER ONE

'WAIT! Don't go.'

The command stopped Elizabeth mid-stride in her dash through the downpour to her car. She spun around, her car keys held in her clenched fist so that they extended stiffly out between her knuckles. There had been no one else in the women's toilet and now the vacant parking area mocked her sense of hearing. Her imagination was playing tricks on her—no one was around. There was only the heavy rain, and the high-pitched whine of tyres speeding past on the rain-slicked highway that bordered the rest area. Normally on a June evening there would be hordes of tourists taking advantage of this stopping-place on the inter-state between Denver and Colorado Springs. The late hour in combination with the heavy rainfall must have driven the tourists off the roads early this evening. Elizabeth shivered, as much from the unexpected isolation as from the wet, chilly weather.

Her key was already in the car door when the faint voice called out again. 'Hear me? Need help. Don't go. Please.'

Despite the last word, the voice conveyed a sense of giving orders. Elizabeth stood irresolute, her out-stretched arm motionless. A swift glance around the area told her that she was still alone. Someone's radio . . . a quirk of the storm transmitting snatches of some programme. Quickly she unlocked the door and started to get in.

'Please. Help. I can't...'

The voice was unquestionably weaker. With the last words, Elizabeth had pin-pointed their origin. The calls were coming from the men's side of the small brick building. In vain she prayed for just one car to pull off the interstate. The clever thing to do would be to drive on to Monument and call the police; she tossed her handbag on to the car seat. On the other hand, if the man needed immediate assistance... She swung her legs from under the wheel. Should she leave her keys in the ignition in case she had to make a quick getaway? What if the call for help was merely a ruse to steal her car? She compromised by leaving the door open and holding the ignition key ready in her hand.

Looking anxiously beyond the lighted parking area into the black picnic area behind her, she edged towards the small building, pausing midway beneath the sheltered information area. 'What's the matter?'

'Thank goodness. Afraid you...leave, too.'

Suddenly Elizabeth remembered the car which had sped from the rest area as she'd entered. 'Perhaps the driver went for help.' If only he had, she prayed.

'Didn't want...get involved.'

The voice was filled with contempt, but over the contempt Elizabeth sensed a man fighting to maintain an iron control. Over what? She ran across the open area and halted beneath the extended roof of the small building. Fingers near the floor held the door to the men's toilet open a slit. Her skin crawled at the thought of going inside. 'Can you come out here?'

'Lady, if could...would I...in here? No time...act...dizzy blonde.'

'How do you know I'm blonde?' The inane question met with the groan it deserved. Elizabeth sensed that the man's iron control was beginning to crumble around the edges. The fingers gave a spasmodic twitch and then were still. The door pressed closed against them.

'Are you all right?' she asked. There was no answer. After one more unanswered prayer that someone else miraculously appear, Elizabeth swallowed hard and pushed open the heavy door. A man lay face down on the floor. Elizabeth sank to her knees beside him; the cold floor was reassuring to her trembling legs. 'You can't just lie there,' she said, the merest wobble in her voice.

The man's face was turned towards her. He opened one eye. The iris was a deep, dark blue. 'Got better idea?'

'Can you walk?'

'Hell. Dance jig, lady. Help...up.' His eye closed as if he were exhausted by the effort to speak.

Elizabeth stood up and stepped over him, wincing as she saw the red stain on the man's arm and shoulder. Stooping down, she grasped his uninjured arm and tried to hoist him up, but the sheer weight of his upper body pulled her down to her knees. She knelt there on all fours. 'You'll have to help,' she panted.

'Somebody else.'

'There isn't anybody else.' Tugging, she managed to pull his arm over her shoulders. 'Hang on and try to stand up.' Breathing heavily she fought to pull them both upright on their knees. The string of swear words coming from the man told her how painful the manoeuvre was for him, but if she stopped to allow him to rest they'd lose what little ground they'd gained. 'We're going to stand now,' she instructed. 'Quit being such a sissy and try harder.' Hadn't she heard that anger gave people strength?

'Sympathetic bitch,' he murmured, his fingers digging painfully into her shoulders as he struggled to rise.

'Forget the sweet talk and try harder,' Elizabeth ground out through clenched teeth. One arm clutched tightly around his waist, she grabbed on to the nearest sink and pulled them both up, a protracted process that was exceedingly painful for the man, judging by the words that poured from his lips and the moisture beading on his brow. Upright at last, they sagged as one against the sink. Elizabeth gave him a brief respite. 'OK,' she said briskly. 'Now, a little hike to the car.'

He opened both eyes. 'Want . . . kill me?'

'If I wanted to do that, I'd leave you lying here.'

His body shuddered with a painful sigh. 'Let's go.'

Cars flashed heedlessly by out on the highway. Elizabeth no longer held any hope that a passing motorist would come to her rescue. Their pace was slow and shuffling, the short distance to the car magnified a hundredfold by the weight of the weakened man leaning on her. The rain was cold, her clothes soaked, her hair plastered to her face. The man swore as he tripped over a crack in the pavement, his loss of balance almost causing her to fall. 'Sorry,' he said.

'What happened?' Maybe talking would distract him from his pain.

'Two creeps. Wanted money. Refused. Shot me.' The succinct explanation was punctuated with groans.

Elizabeth's stomach dipped alarmingly—the bullet might have hit a vital organ. She shouldn't have moved him. 'Shot?' Hopefully he wouldn't notice how her voice quivered.

'Shoulder. Fell. Hit my head. Sink. Blacked out.'

Relief poured through Elizabeth's veins. No vital organs. 'Here's my car,' she said thankfully.

She had to prop him against the cold, wet metal while she reached in through the open door and unlocked the back. He was already so wet that a little more dampness hardly mattered. More swear-words ripped from his lips as she manoeuvred him into a reclining position on the back seat. Stretching over him, she snapped the seatbelt snugly around him. Backing out of the car, she happened to glance down at her blouse. A dark stain spread down the side. Elizabeth swallowed hard against a rising panic. One look confirmed her worst suspicions: their exertions had disturbed his wound. Her few paper tissues were of little use and she searched her car in vain for something to use as a bandage. If she could get his shirt off him... 'Can you sit up?'

No reply. It was hopeless—he'd blacked out again. She tried to lift him to remove his shirt but his body was a dead weight. Women always tore up their petticoats in the movies. Unfortunately, she wasn't wearing a petticoat. With the barest twinge of regret she took off her white eyelet blouse. It was probably already stained beyond repair. Quickly she wrung the rainwater out of the fabric as best she could, folded the blouse into a fat square and pressed it against the shoulder wound. She needed something to secure it... Seatbelts. But how in the world could she get one free?

The man opened his eyes and stared blankly at her. 'You...angel?'

At least he was conscious. She put his hand over the makeshift pad. 'Hold this,' she ordered, giving up on trying to free a seatbelt.

His eyes flickered shut. Elizabeth wanted to shake him. The pad against his wound wouldn't do any good if it weren't pressed tightly. She slipped out of her bra.

'Not Michael or Gabriel.' Glazed eyes were locked on her breasts.

She uttered a short laugh. 'Be careful. Get too fresh and I'll slug you no matter how hurt you are.' She knew that she was only talking to keep her fears at bay. She didn't like the wide-eyed, staring look in the man's eyes. What did she know about concussions?

'Thought angels...men.' His uninjured hand brushed against one breast. 'Woman. Soft. Silky. And warm. Very warm.' His palm slid over her breast, his thumb curling around the sensitive tip.

In spite of herself, Elizabeth felt a rush of tingling sensation swell her nipple. Hastily she moved his hand back to his side. 'Behave yourself or I'll leave you here.'

'Can't.' The man chortled softly. 'Angel. My angel. Right?'

'Yes,' she agreed, to humour him. She cut the straps off the bra and tied all the pieces end to end. Leaning over him, she worked the improvised rope beneath his body.

'Smell good, Angel.'

She sat up and tied her blouse tightly against the wound. 'There. That's the best I can do.'

'Angel. Hold me. Hurts.' His voice rose with the last word.

Elizabeth slipped to her knees on the floor of the car. Gently she cradled him in her arms. He turned and pressed his face between her breasts. 'I need to get you to a doctor,' she said.

His free hand clutched convulsively at her skirt. 'Minute.'

'All right.' A lock of black, wavy hair had fallen down over his forehead and she smoothed it back. Only one eyebrow was visible. It was thick and black. A deep line was gouged from his well-shaped nose to lips thinned in pain. His jutting jaw, clenched against the pain, was dark. She brushed her hand against it— afternoon whiskers scratched her skin. The slight movement must have roused him. She felt his eyelashes whisper against her breasts as he opened his eyes.

'Angel. All dark!' Panic was in his voice.

'It's all right, I'm here.' What an inane thing to say. Nothing was all right. She had to get him to a hospital.

'Cold, Angel. Warm me.'

Was it her imagination or was his voice weaker? 'I need to get you to the hospital. I'll turn on the car heater. Is that OK?' He didn't answer. She laid his head back gently on the seat. His eyes were closed. Her heart skipped a beat before she saw the regular rise and fall of his chest. He was unconscious again. There was no more time to waste.

Once outside the car she quickly yanked her skirt up to her armpits, giving silent thanks that she'd worn a skirt with an elastic waistband. At least she wouldn't be arrested for indecent exposure, even if she did look ridiculous. Not that it mattered: all that mattered was the man in the back seat. The man whose face's imprint was burned into her skin.

Once on the interstate the windscreen wipers fought to keep up with the heavy deluge of rain. As they swept back and forth they seemed to be urging her on: 'Hurry, hurry, hurry.' She glanced at the man in her rear-view mirror. He was still unconscious. Talk to him, that was what she was supposed to do. Talk to him to keep him from slipping totally over the edge.

'You're lucky that I came along; normally I never stop there. It was all that coffee I drank at the Denver airport.' Hours and hours at Stapleton, waiting for Sandy's delayed plane to finally depart. 'This has not been the best day of my life. First I had a flat tyre just outside of Colorado Springs. I can tell you about good Samaritans: they are few and far between, believe me. I had the spare almost on before a highway patrolman stopped to help me.'

She glanced down at her blue chambray skirt. The black, greasy smear would probably never come out. 'And you can bet that Sandy saw it first thing. If you could have seen the smug look on her face as she stood there, not a hair out of place, wearing this super-chic silk suit, it would have made you sick. It did me.' And why ever she had agreed to meet Sandy when the other was between planes at Stapleton was a mystery. 'What made her think that I was the least bit interested in her wonderful job in television and the fantastic men that pursue her back in Washington, DC? I thought I'd scream before she finally left. If I'd had to listen to one more name-dropping story or hear about her dating one more super, terrific guy who looks exactly like some movie star, I'd... You wouldn't believe how she goes on and on and... I don't know why I went up there——'

'Why did you?'

The voice from the back seat made her jump. In cataloguing her grievances, she'd almost forgotten her passenger. 'You're awake,' she said. He sounded more lucid this time. 'Are you warm enough?'

'No. Keep talking. Helps,' he added, almost grudgingly. 'Who's Sandy?'

'A good friend. We——'

'Not . . . good,' he interrupted.

Elizabeth gave a little shrug, acknowledging the truth of his comment. 'It's been a long time. In high school we were best friends. But that was six years ago and we've gone our separate ways since then. I didn't realise until today just exactly how separate our separate ways were. I felt as if we were acting out the Country Mouse and the City Mouse—needless to say, I was the Country Mouse. OK, you don't need to say it. I know. I was jealous of her. She made her life sound so exciting and glamorous while mine sounded so humdrum in comparison. It's hard to compete with someone who breakfasts with Congressmen and lunches with television celebrities. I mean, shoving a banana down Hewie's throat is hardly anyone's idea of a power breakfast.' She looked in the mirror again. His eyes were closed, while lines of pain were etched deeply across his face. 'You awake?'

'Yes. Go on.' The words shot out from between clenched teeth.

'I probably sound like a whiner, when the truth is that I adore Hewie. I wouldn't trade a hundred breakfasts with Congressmen for one of his smiles. Spring fever must have come late for me this year. I adore the kids, I really do. It's just that, listening to Sandy and knowing that she was free to do whatever she wanted to do whenever she wanted to do it——'

'Kids. How many?'

'Seven. Well, five really. Abigail and Georgia say that I can't count them. And the baby isn't due until Christmas. I'm hoping for a little girl but Chan says that we have enough girls and he wants another boy, to balance things out. I guess he's right, but when I think of all those adorable dresses that Anna Belle designed... She was so sure that Hewie was going to be a girl. I warned her that she ought to make something blue, but when Anna Belle makes up her mind...'

She let out a sigh of relief: the hospital at last. She'd never talked so much in her life. She'd be embarrassed to death if she didn't know that this man would be lucky to remember her in the morning, much less remember her rambling confidences. Driving up to the emergency entrance, she jumped from the car and ran inside. The response was immediate and the injured man was quickly and efficiently removed from her car.

Elizabeth stood awkwardly to one side as the hospital attendants strapped the man to a narrow trolley. There was nothing else for her to do, but she felt that to walk away now was to abandon him.

One of the attendants gave her a sympathetic look. 'We'll take him now, miss.' They started towards the doors.

'Thank you.' There would be questions inside before she could go home—not that she could tell them much. She turned to go back and move her car.

'Angel?' The voice was querulous. He tried to push himself up.

She hurried to his side before he could injure himself more. His groping hand found hers as she kept pace with the moving bed. 'You'll be OK now; we're at the hospital.' The lines of pain on his face seemed to have deepened.

Inside the hospital the attendants stopped before another set of double doors. 'You'll have to wait here, miss.'

'Yes.' Stirred by a sudden impulse, Elizabeth leaned down and kissed the injured man softly on his cheek. 'Good luck, and take care of yourself.' She tugged her hand from his grasp.

'Angel?' Pain-filled blue eyes sought her out.

From the corner of her eye she was aware of one of the attendants making an impatient movement. She ignored him. 'I have to go now,' she gently told the injured man.

'I want to . . . thanks.' His body went limp and his eyes closed.

The attendants swept him from the hallway. Double doors that swung silently back into place marked their passage.

'Any time,' Elizabeth said.

'Tommy, I don't want to talk about it any more,' Elizabeth said. Her younger brother had teased her unmercifully ever since the night she'd arrived home wearing little more than a filthy, rain-drenched skirt. She'd been naïve to believe that she could sneak into the house before anyone noticed; just as she'd been naïve in thinking that her little exploit could be kept from the newspapers. Fortunately the family had united behind her and refused to give interviews, so her newsworthiness had quickly faded. If only her family would drop the subject. Elizabeth was tired of the role of heroine; and she said so as she dunked a squirming Barney into the sudsy water.

'You'd think the guy would come by or telephone you or something, to thank you,' Tommy said. He grimaced as the small beagle splashed water all over him.

Elizabeth had no trouble pin-pointing the identity of 'the guy'. 'He sent roses. Barney, quit wriggling.'

'Flowers—big deal. You saved his life. You rotten mutt...' This last was addressed to the dog, who'd redoubled his efforts to escape his bath.

'I doubt that. The paper said that it was just a flesh wound.'

'Yeah, but he lost buckets of blood, and it was a pretty chilly night, even for June. A little more gratitude would be nice.'

'What did you have in mind? A million dollars? Stop your howling, Barney. It's not my fault that you tipped over the garbage can and rolled in some nasty, smelly old food.'

'How 'bout a couple of his oil wells?' Tommy spat over his shoulder as the dog showered him once more.

'They're not exactly his,' Elizabeth pointed out.

'Just the same, he's not exactly a pauper. All those years with that oil company working in Saudi Arabia—those guys make big bucks. Gimme the towel. I'll take Barney inside and dry him off.'

Blessed peace descended on the back garden as Tommy disappeared into the house with the yelping dog. Barney made more noise than a dog twice his size. Elizabeth dumped the abandoned bath-water over the grass and hosed off the plastic tub. The warm June afternoon sun felt good on her bare arms. A small butterfly, the same creamy yellow as the patch of columbine it floated from, danced in the spray of the hose. It fluttered closer to Elizabeth and then quickly darted away. No wonder—she reeked of dog. Her mystery man would hardly say she smelled good now.

Her mystery man. Only he wasn't a mystery any more: the mugging had been front-page news and she knew all about Andrew T. Harcourt. Only thirty-one years old, he had won acclaim from his employers and his peers for his brilliance and hard work. As a petroleum engineer he'd lived a nomadic life, and the newspaper had made much of the irony of a man returning safely from wild outposts far beyond the borders of civilisation only to be mugged on the highways of Colorado. Apparently, Andrew T. Harcourt had returned to the States to spend the summer in the oil company's home office located in Colorado Springs. He'd been to Denver on company business on the day of the crime. On his way home, he'd heard odd sounds from his car and had pulled off at the rest-stop to check under the bonnet. He'd found nothing wrong and had gone into the men's bathroom to wash his hands. Beyond that his memory was hazy, but the doctor said that that was to be expected because of his head injury. Someone had informed him of Elizabeth's involvement because she had received flowers, with a very polite, formal thankyou. Addressed to Elizabeth Asher. Not to Angel. Elizabeth shifted the hose to water the boxes of geraniums that surrounded the patio. There had been a picture in the newspaper, a studio portrait, that had given little hint of his physique. She was five feet, five inches tall and he'd loomed over her, putting his height at above six feet. Fortunately he was on the wiry side, almost thin, or she'd never have been able to get him to her car.

Thin, but there was nothing wrong with his shoulders. She hadn't needed the photograph to prompt her memory. His eyes had been almost all pupil in the aftermath of concussion, but the iris that rimmed the black had been a deep blue. The dark hair, the strong, unshaven jaw. The rasp of his stubby whiskers against her bare skin.

Mentally she gave herself an impatient shake. Fate had brought her to the right place at the right time to help the man. Her role in his life was played out. There was no reason for them to meet again. She didn't require thanks for doing something that any decent person would have done. OK, she admitted to curiosity. Wasn't it the Chinese who said that if you saved a person's life, then that life belonged to you? Not that she wanted his life. She just wanted to know more about the kind of person this Andrew T. Harcourt was. What would he do with this life that Tommy insisted she'd saved? She wanted to know the rest of the story.

'You're drowning those geraniums.'

Elizabeth turned with a start. She hadn't heard Tommy come back outside. One look at him and she burst out laughing. 'Who had the bath, you or Barney?'

'You don't look so elegant yourself.'

'At least I don't look like a drowned rat.'

'Oh yeah?' With a quick movement, Tommy jerked the hose from Elizabeth and turned the nozzle in her direction.

The shock of the cold water made her gasp. 'You beast! You dirty, rotten...' Disregarding the stream

of water pouring over her, Elizabeth plunged towards
Tommy. He pranced backwards, taunting her with
words and holding the hose just out of her reach. With
a sudden lunge, she captured the nozzle. Tommy took
one look at her vengeful face and sped off around
the house, well aware that he was running for his life.

'You can run and you can flee, but you'll never get
away from me,' Elizabeth chanted, pointing the hose
nozzle away from her as she rounded the corner of
the house.

What happened next was as if a bad dream were
playing in slow motion before her eyes. Georgia,
hearing the yells and seeing her brother running at
top speed around the corner, immediately grasped the
connection between these two occurrences and
promptly stepped behind the protection of the high
fence bordering the back garden—abandoning
without a qualm the man who was following her. The
man who received squarely in the middle of his face
the full force of the water spraying from the hose.
The hose held and aimed by Elizabeth.

'What the hell——?'

'Oh, no!'

'You could at least point the damned thing somewhere else.'

'Oh.' In her shock Elizabeth had failed to realise
that she was standing like a dunce, the hose still
pointing directly ahead, if a little lower. 'Sorry.' She
dropped the nozzle. Like a twisting, writhing snake,
the rubber hose contorted its way to the ground,
spraying the man at least three more times in the
process. Finally it lay on the ground, water gushing
from the nozzle to form a small river that flowed over
the tops of the man's loafers. Caught between horror

and hysteria, Elizabeth was unable to swallow a small gurgle of laughter.

'Very amusing, I'm sure,' the man snapped.

Tommy was long gone, and Georgia had taken advantage of the confusion to quietly slip away. Elizabeth wished that she could disappear as easily. 'I'm sorry. I didn't mean to laugh.' She bit the inside of her cheek to hold back any more unsuitable laughter. Water-drenched strings of black hair hung low above stormy blue eyes. He was furious and she couldn't blame him. But still, he did look ludicrous standing there, dripping wet, a soggy package in his arm, his white shirt tinted red by the soaked bow, the sling on his arm...

'Oh.' She sat abruptly down on the pavement, right in the middle of the water gushing from the hose. The shock of the icy water propelled her immediately back to her feet.

The man's lips twitched. 'You can't be Elizabeth Asher.'

'Why can't I?'

'After talking with the hospital staff, the police and the newspaper reporters, I'd pictured you a little differently.'

'Oh?'

'More along the lines of a brave, brawny Amazon. A woman who'd defied the night and the elements and the evil forces of crime to deliver me to safety.' An air of disbelief accompanied the comprehensive survey made by dark blue eyes. 'I'm Andrew Harcourt, by the way.'

'I know who you are. I was the conscious one, remember?' She wished that he were unconscious now—long enough for her to escape. She didn't need a mirror to tell her that her hair hung in unattractive wet strands down her back, that her soaked clothing clung to her body and that her arms were covered with dog hairs. Rivulets of water ran down the back of her legs from her sopping shorts. It would be difficult to picture anyone who looked less like a heroine.

An assessment that Andrew T. Harcourt obviously agreed with, if the supercilious look on his face was anything to go by. Elizabeth repeated his middle initial contemptuously to herself, as if it were a talisman that would protect her from this man and his blatant disapproval of her. Without thinking, she blurted out, 'What's the "T" stand for?'

'None of your business.'

Elizabeth arched one eyebrow in enquiry. 'That bad?'

'What the hell difference does it make?'

She shrugged. 'Just curious.'

His eyes narrowed thoughtfully as he scanned her body once more. 'Are you sure you're Elizabeth Asher?'

'Would you like to see my driver's licence?'

His lips thinned at the hint of saccharin in her voice. 'Here,' he said, holding out the sodden package. 'I'm afraid that yours were beyond repair, but my mother thought these were fairly similar.' When Elizabeth just stared at him in surprise, he impatiently thrust the package into her hands. 'Here. They're yours.'

The package was soft and lightweight. Curiously, Elizabeth ripped away the wet paper. Folded inside, protected by the heavy wrapping paper, was a white blouse. 'Oh,' she said in delight, 'you didn't have to...' She shook out the blouse. The realisation that something had been hidden within the folds came too late.

A lacy white brassière floated down to drape over one bare foot, its straps sinking into the puddle Elizabeth stood in.

Her gaze was irresistibly drawn to the face of the man standing in front of her. An expression of unholy glee glinted fleetingly in his eyes before his lids dropped. He studied the garment at their feet. A slight breath of air rippled the surface of the water and gave embarrassing shape to the white fabric. Elizabeth snatched it up. 'You didn't have to——'

'Neither did you, but you did. And I'm grateful. Roses seemed an absurdly inadequate gesture of thanks, but I didn't want to insult you by offering money.' He glanced at the muddy scrap that she was endeavouring to hide inside the white blouse. 'Replacing your clothing is the least I could do. Do you mind if I ask one question?'

Elizabeth eyed him warily. Did he remember calling her his angel? Or her comforting him? What if he'd misread her actions? 'What?'

'Why did you help me?'

The unexpected question shocked her. 'You were hurt. You needed help.'

'That's it?'

'What else could there be?' She drew her brows together in a fierce frown. 'Are you accusing me of some ulterior motive? I suppose you think that I expect a reward. Haven't you ever heard of the milk of human kindness? What do you think I am? An ambulance chaser? Let me remind you that I didn't come looking for you, Mr Andrew T. Harcourt. You came to my house. And now you can just leave. Of all the disgusting, loathsome things . . . to accuse me of something so vile . . .' Holding her back ramrod-straight, she looked him squarely in the eye. 'I'll accept the clothes because that's only fair. The roses are dead, or I'd give them back to you. As for you——'

He was destined never to know, because at that moment Mai Tai came tearing through the open gate. To the Siamese cat, the tall man must have seemed the answer to a feline prayer because, without an instant's hesitation, she climbed up his body to sit on his shoulder. As she hissed behind her, the object of her wrath charged through the gate. Elizabeth gave a shrill cry and the large grey dog applied the brakes to all four enormous feet. Unfortunately, the paws failed to grab hold on the wet concrete and, his nails desperately scrambling, the dog skidded directly towards Andrew Harcourt. The man's reactions were incredibly fast. Turning his injured arm away from the dog, he threw a body check that stopped the dog in mid-stride and flung him back towards Elizabeth. Once again she found herself on her behind in a cold puddle of water.

Only this time she was holding an armful of grey, furry dog. Sam liked the situation as little as Elizabeth, especially after he spied the object of his chase. Elizabeth felt the dog's muscles gathering to spring and she shouted, 'Get rid of Mai Tai. I can't hold Sam much longer.' The words were no sooner shouted than the prophecy came true. Uttering an enormous howl, Sam sprang from her grasp. This time Andrew Harcourt was too slow. The cat leaped gracefully from his shoulder to the top of the fence just as the dog careered into the man. They fell to the ground with a flurry of arms and legs and a great deal of splashing. This was a new game to Sam and he immediately barked sharply in delight. Elizabeth's heart stopped as she saw the still, supine form beneath the dog's quivering body. A steady, muffled stream of swear-words set her heart beating again. She waded through the water on her knees and, grabbing Sam by his collar, yanked him off his new-found playmate. Luckily, at that moment, Mai Tai protested vociferously Sam's abandoning their game, and the dog enthusiastically returned to the chase. As he departed his heavy tail whacked Elizabeth across the face, knocking her over again.

Andrew Harcourt lay on his back in the puddle beside her. His eyes were shut but his lips moved unceasingly in a fierce, low mumble that Elizabeth was grateful she couldn't decipher. 'Are you OK?' she asked.

'Why wouldn't I be? A nice summer day, a cool dip in the pool—what more could any man ask?'

Elizabeth sat up. 'Let me help you.'

'Don't touch me.'

In spite of the snapped command, she felt a twinge of remorse at the grimace of pain that crossed his face as he pulled himself to an upright position. 'I'm sorry,' she said.

'I'm sorry, too. Sorry I didn't mail the package to you. Why couldn't the muggers have run into you instead of me? You'd have had them begging to be arrested.' Furiously he made futile efforts to wring the water from his trousers.

Elizabeth rose to her feet and rescued her new clothing from the puddle. 'I don't blame you for being annoyed.'

'Annoyed? Annoyed! That has to be the understatement of the year.'

She trailed him silently around to the front of the house. There didn't seem to be any words to apologise or to explain away what had happened. His anger was understandable, but at the same time a slight pang of injustice smote her. Drenching him with the hose was admittedly her fault, but he surely couldn't blame the animals' behaviour on her.

A dark blue sedan was parked in the driveway. Andrew Harcourt reached the car and started to walk around to the driver's side, then hesitated a moment before turning back to Elizabeth. 'What happened here...' He paused. 'I shouldn't have said what I said about the muggers. I'm truly grateful for your aid.'

His obvious sincerity went a long way towards dispelling Elizabeth's smouldering resentment. In a belated attempt at hospitality, she said, 'I didn't even offer you anything to drink, Mr Harcourt.'

'Andrew.' The corners of his mouth tilted up. 'I've had enough water, thanks.'

The unexpected smile, full of boyish charm, totally disarmed Elizabeth. She couldn't have prevented the smile that curved her own mouth in response even if she'd wanted to.

Andrew extended his uninjured hand. 'Thank you.'

Elizabeth placed her hand in his. 'You're welcome.' His hand was cool against her skin. Tingling sensations travelled upward from his touch, speeding up the tempo of her heart. Just as it had when he'd touched her that night...touched her so intimately. Did he remember anything about that night? 'Andrew...'

He tugged gently on the hand still imprisoned in his. 'Hmm?'

He was going to kiss her. She dropped her gaze, unable to withstand the intensity of his.

'Oh, Elizabeth,' a voice cooed in her ear, 'I didn't know you had company. I thought I'd take Sam for a walk.'

Elizabeth whirled round. Abigail, a picture in her new lavender dress, posed on the pavement, testing her recently discovered feminine charms upon a new and more worthy victim than her usual college retinue. With innocent and misguided cunning, she had hit upon the excuse of walking the dog in order to bring herself within Andrew's orbit.

All these thoughts flew simultaneously through Elizabeth's mind even as she sensed the danger. 'No!' she hollered, as Sam recognised his new playmate and enthusiastically raised two enormous muddy paws to greet him. Diving for Sam's collar, out of the corner of her eye Elizabeth spotted Laura being towed up the pavement by a gigantic Great Dane, with a small dachshund trotting behind. The front screen-door slammed, and Elizabeth felt it only inevitable that Barney was dashing across the garden to join the fray.

Any notion of kisses fled in the ensuing pandemonium. Finally all was sorted out, a chastened Abigail hauling Sam back into the house while an apologetic Laura dragged her charges down the street. Elizabeth and Andrew were left alone in the front garden. Alone? A sudden premonition gripped Elizabeth, and she looked down just in time to see Barney lift his leg and anoint Andrew's trousers. This final absurdity proved too much for her deplorable sense of humour. She sank to her knees on the grass and dissolved into laughter.

CHAPTER TWO

'ELIZABETH, it's the strangest thing, but I swear that there's a man over there hiding from us. He keeps ducking behind pillars or other dancers every time he sees us. I've never seen him before in my life.'

'Dance me around so that I can see.'

Vince obediently did as commanded. 'See him?'

'No.'

'He's with that tall, sexy brunette. She's wearing a scrap of red fabric.'

'Aha. Now I see how you noticed them. Oops—he saw me looking and whirled about before I got a good look. Now I can only see his back. Good heavens, there's less to the front of that dress than the back. Vince, how can I see the man if you do that?' she wailed.

'You shouldn't have mentioned the front of her dress.' Obligingly he turned her once again so that she could view the couple. 'It truly is a marvel of engineering. How in the world do you suppose it stays up?'

'How would I know? I'm hardly that well-endowed.'

Vince grinned down at her. 'Sorry. I wasn't thinking.'

'You're incorrigible.'

'Don't you mean safe?'

'That, too,' she admitted. 'Don't you ever worry that some day I might decide that the ever-so-charming Vince Hunter might make me the perfect husband?'

'Nope. In the first place, we both know I wouldn't, and, in the second, you're totally content playing den mother. Which makes us the perfect couple. The man who won't be tied down and the woman who already is.'

Totally content. Once she would have agreed with him. But now... Something was missing in her life. Ever since that day she'd met Sandy in Denver she'd been unsettled. Could she have been jealous of Sandy's glamorous life after all?

'Weird,' Vince hissed in her ear. 'I'm trying to get closer to them but he's dancing her away just as fast as he can. I'm sure he's trying to avoid us.'

'Are you positive that you don't know the brunette? Maybe he's a worried husband.'

'The brunettes I date don't come to swank charity balls like this one. If they did, I wouldn't have to bring you.'

'Thanks.'

'You know what I mean. If I brought one of my usual dates to an affair like this, they'd be making out the wedding invitation list the next day.'

'What would you do without me?' Elizabeth mocked.

'Shoot myself. Got them,' he added in satisfaction. 'He's backed himself into a corner and can't get away. Watch this.' The final words were whispered into Elizabeth's ear.

She couldn't help grinning in response. Vince and his games. She knew very well that this whole charade was designed to enable him to meet the brunette. The grin was still on her lips as Vince led her through an intricate series of dance steps that ended up with her whirling breathlessly into another man's arms. 'You!'

'Miss Asher.' Andrew Harcourt gravely inclined his head.

Elizabeth couldn't resist the impulse to look down.

'No dogs are allowed on the dance floor, fortunately,' he said.

Obviously he had no trouble deciphering her thoughts. 'But you thought you'd keep a safe distance, just in case,' she countered.

His smile didn't reach his eyes. 'It seemed prudent. There's always the fountain of champagne.'

'Coward.' The throat being cleared at her side reminded her of Vince and she drew his hand through her arm. 'Vince, this is Andrew T. Harcourt.' Deliberately she emphasised the middle initial. 'Mr Harcourt, this is Vince Hunter.'

'T?' Vince asked, shaking the outstretched hand.

'Miss Asher's little joke,' he said, glaring at Elizabeth.

She smiled innocently back at him, relishing the feeling that she'd annoyed him. The angry words that had marked his departure the other day still rankled. Not everything that had happened had been her fault. She switched her attention to the brunette. 'Hello. I'm Elizabeth Asher and this gentleman panting at your feet is Vince Hunter.'

'Elizabeth Asher. You're our little heroine.' The pleasant timbre of the low, throaty voice robbed the words of any sting.

Vince looked from Elizabeth to Andrew, comprehension slowly dawning on his face. 'You're the guy Elizabeth picked up.'

'In a manner of speaking,' Andrew said. 'Allow me to introduce Bunny Irving.'

'Bunny. Wonderful to meet you. How about dancing with me, so that you can tell me how a beautiful Bunny like you has managed to escape the predatory instincts of a great Hunter like myself all this time?'

'Don't frown,' Elizabeth chided Andrew as he watched Vince sweep his date away from under his nose. 'Vince is totally harmless. Perhaps your irritation is based less on losing Bunny than on being stuck with me. Not very flattering. I promise not to trip you on the dance floor.'

'Would you mind terribly sitting this one out?'

'Certainly not. In fact, I'll do you one better. I'll excuse myself to the powder-room and then you won't have to bother with me at all.' Indignantly she turned away, blinking unexpected tears from her eyes.

'Miss Asher—Elizabeth . . .'

She stopped and glared down at the hand grasping her elbow as if it were a loathsome cockroach. 'The trouble with men is that they can't laugh at themselves.'

'The trouble with women is that they jump to conclusions.'

That brought her head up and around. 'Meaning?'

'Tonight is the first time that my arm has been out of the sling, and my shoulder aches. That's why I prefer not to dance right now.'

Elizabeth was instantly contrite. 'You shouldn't have come, in your condition.'

'After what I've been through lately, a mere dance didn't seem so dangerous. I should have remembered that danger can lie in unexpected places.' He paused.

'Would you care to step outside for a breath of fresh air?'

'Won't Bunny mind?'

He looked back towards the dance floor. 'Your friend seems to be keeping her adequately entertained.' A hand pressed against the small of her back guided her around the perimeter of the large ballroom. Dresses of every colour and variety were in elegant contrast to the black and white evening-wear sported by the gentlemen. Men were drinking and smoking in the carpeted hallway, their low-pitched voices and tinkling ice cubes barely audible above the catchy melody being played in the ballroom.

Her companion showed no inclination towards speech, and Elizabeth hummed along with the band. Andrew led the way in the direction of a low brick wall and rested his elbows on it, looking up into the night. The sky was brilliantly clear, the stars twinkling jewels in a setting of blue velvet.

'The Big Dipper is easy to see tonight,' he said.

Elizabeth glanced over at him. Light spilled out from the ballroom windows, bathing him in a golden glow. He wore his dinner-jacket with an air of casual aplomb that seemed to boast a familiarity with formal affairs such as this; but surely, with his job, he'd be more comfortable in work clothes and a hard hat. Suddenly she was curious to know more about him. 'The newspaper said that you've been all over the world. What's it like living in such exotic places?'

'Different. Not necessarily better or worse. The differences are what make living in foreign countries so fascinating. So much history and culture to learn.' He turned and leaned back against the wall.

'Do you ever miss America?'

'Occasionally. A person grows up accustomed to certain patterns of living, customs, manners, even certain foods. I admit to sitting in the desert sometimes and dreaming of a nice, cold beer. And,' he gazed up at the sky, 'there have been times out on a platform in the North Sea when I've longed for the warmth of the desert. Most of the time, however, I'm too busy to be pining away for something I can't have. Besides, the world is smaller today than ever before. TV satellites beam American football games all over the world, and American fast-food joints are on almost every corner.'

'Oh, well, as long as you have the necessities of life.'

'Absolutely.' He straightened up and looked down at her, his teeth glinting in the light as he smiled. 'When I'm here, that other world seems like a dream. When I'm there . . .' his hand cradled her chin, tipping her face up ' . . . this will seem like a dream.'

He hesitated a moment, but when Elizabeth made no move to pull away he bent his head, his mouth warmly covering hers. She could taste the wine on his lips. There was no other contact between them except for their touching lips and his fingers softly caressing her cheek. His breath was warm against her skin. Music poured from the ballroom to accompany the sound of his breathing. Andrew's fingers slid over her face and slipped between them, parting them. He traced the outline of her lips. She hoped he couldn't feel them trembling.

'What is it about you?' he murmured. 'You hold a mysterious attraction for me that defies all logic.' He studied her face intently as if the answer to his confusion lay there. 'All I know of you tells me that you are frivolous and irresponsible. If there's a serious bone in your body, it's well hidden, and yet . . .'

The night air acquired a desolate chill. Elizabeth took a step backwards. 'It can't be good for you to be standing out here in the cold. We'd better go back inside.'

'No.' Hands on her shoulders pulled her back close to him. 'Not until I understand. Reason tells me to run and hide when you're around——'

'As you did tonight,' she interjected.

His hands slid across her shoulders to curve gently around her, his fingers laced together behind her neck. 'I knew the instant you entered the ballroom this evening. It was as if you'd sent out some signal, but I realise that you didn't even know I was here. What happened that night?'

Elizabeth stiffened. 'Surely you've been told?'

'Nothing that explains this compulsion I have to hold you, to be held by you. Something in my subconscious seems to overshadow my rational behaviour whenever you're around.'

She concentrated on his black bow-tie, cursing the compassionate feelings that had prompted her to cradle him in her arms when he'd been hurt. 'I found you, helped you into my car and drove you to the hospital. That's all.' She shrugged. 'Anything else that you imagine . . . well, don't forget you had a severe concussion.'

When she would have moved away, his grip tightened, giving her no opportunity to deny him. Fingers pressed against her scalp held her immobile as his mouth descended once more. No gentle, tentative kiss this time. He aggressively parted her lips, his firm, thrusting tongue demanding her partici-

pation. A hand moved down her back to her hips,
holding her snug against his body. Heat from his hand
burned her skin through the fabric of her dress. Deep
within her an unfamiliar pressure began to build.

Andrew nibbled on the fullness of her bottom lip,
an activity so charged with sensuous pleasure that the
tiny core of anger his earlier words had aroused totally
faded away to be replaced by arousal of a different
nature. His lips burned their way over her skin, before
he pressed his mouth against the rapidly beating pulse
at the base of her neck. Blood throbbed in her ears,
blotting out the music from the ballroom. Her breath
came in short pants, each breath filled with Andrew's
masculine scent. He traced the outlines of her hip-
bone with one hand while the other lightly trailed
down the front of her dress. Her body was raised to
such heights of sensitivity that even through the layers
of fabric she could feel her breasts begin to swell, the
peaks hardening with desire.

Suddenly his arms went around her shoulders and
he hugged her tightly to him, his lips pressing fiercely
against the softness of her mouth. As if he were memorising the feel of her, the taste of her lips. Then he
wrenched his mouth from hers and dropped his arms.

Elizabeth was confused. The swift, unexpected loss
of his body heat chilled her skin and her lips ached
with the pain of abandonment. Then she realised that
the music had stopped. The murmur of approaching
voices told her that others were seeking fresh air.

Andrew was wiping his mouth with his handkerchief. 'Forgive me.' His voice was distant and formal.
'For a moment, I forgot about your husband.'

Elizabeth gaped at him in astonishment. 'I'm not
married.'

'But you were.' His voice was filled with conviction.

'No, never.'

He frowned, as if searching for an elusive memory. 'Strange, I could have sworn . . . it suddenly popped into my mind that you were married, as if I knew it.' He shook his head slowly. 'I must be thinking of someone else. There was a baby—Louie, or something like that.' He brushed his hand across his face. 'These damned memory lapses. The doctor warned me they might occur. Fragments of memories drift by, tantalising me, but I can't grasp the whole memory.'

Elizabeth caught her breath, torn between pity and an unwillingness to divulge all that had happened. Perhaps she could tell him enough to set his mind at ease. 'I told you about my nephew, Hewie, that night.'

His attention caught, he stared at her. 'What else?' he demanded.

'I don't remember all I said. Mostly I was talking to try and take your mind off the pain. I remember telling you about my family; the kids. You wanted to know how many.' She looked up at him. 'You probably thought that I meant they were my kids. That's why you thought I was married.'

'What kids are they?'

'My brothers and sisters.'

He leaned back against the wall. 'Tell me about your family. Maybe that will help my memory.'

Confident that it wasn't memories of her family that he was trying to recall, Elizabeth welcomed the safe topic. 'There's eight of us. Chan, he's the oldest. Then me. Next is Abigail. She was the one in the lavender dress.'

'Walking Sam,' he said drily.

Elizabeth nodded. 'Then comes Tommy. He was the one I intended to drench. Then Georgia.'

'The one who didn't warn me.'

She ignored that remark. 'Next is Laura. She has a job caring for some neighbourhood dogs this summer.'

'Thus explaining the Great Dane and the dachshund.'

'Uh-huh. Susan is ten, and finally comes Julia, the baby of the family at seven. That's all of us. Unless of course you count Hewie.'

'By all means, count Hewie. Who is he?'

'Chan's little boy. Chan and his wife, Paige, are living with us temporarily. They are building a house and it didn't get finished when it was supposed to, and their other lease ran out. Paige hasn't been feeling well, with the new baby on the way, so everyone thought it best that they move in with us for a while.'

'No parents?'

'Of course, one of each. Did you think we sprang from the sea?'

'Sounds as if your mother has her hands full.'

Elizabeth laughed. 'Not my mother. Me.'

He looked down in surprise. 'What have we here? Cinderella at the ball?'

'Andrew, darling, what are you two doing hiding out here?' Before the question could be answered, Bunny added, 'Vince knows of this terrific heavy metal band playing somewhere tonight. I know you'd hate it, so I'm going with him. You don't mind, do you?' She turned to Elizabeth. 'Vince said you wouldn't. Incidentally, I adore your dress. I've wanted a hand-painted Anna Belle for years, but they're so devastatingly extravagant.'

'Not Cinderella,' Andrew said in Elizabeth's ear.

She ignored him, looking past Bunny. Vince winked at her over the other woman's shoulder. 'Vince.' She said his name as a kind of warning.

'Don't worry, Elizabeth, I know what I'm doing,' Vince said.

'Quit frowning,' Andrew admonished as Vince and Bunny disappeared into the dark night. 'You're the one who assured me that Vince is totally harmless.'

'Ordinarily that's true. According to Vince, there are two types of women in the world: those who want to get married and those who want to have fun. He normally only dates those who want to have fun. To avoid any painful entanglements.'

'Which are you?'

'I'm neither; I'm merely for public consumption. Vince knows I have no intention of marrying, so he's safe with me. And, when it comes to something like this big charity ball where every bigwig in town is present, including Vince's boss, he likes to escort a woman who won't embarrass him.'

'Your friend sounds like a hypocrite and a snob. I can see that I shouldn't have taken your word on his character.'

'Don't tell me that you're worried about Bunny? I'd say that she can take care of herself. I doubt that she's the marrying type any more than Vince is.'

'You're wrong. Bunny is the marrying kind. Twice so far.'

'And you're down for number three,' Elizabeth suggested.

'Like your friend, Vince, I'm not the marrying kind.'

'Does Bunny know that?'

'That, Elizabeth, is none of your business. And now, if you'll allow me to escort you inside, since my date seems to have deserted me I believe I'll leave, too.' After only the barest hesitation, he asked, 'Do you need a ride home?'

There was no mistaking his relief when she coolly rejected his offer. She didn't need to beg a ride from him. Any one of her many friends at the ball would have been happy to oblige her. Even Chan and Paige were present, had she wanted to wait for their departure. But for some reason her enjoyment of the evening had evaporated. As soon as she was certain that Andrew had departed, she called for a taxi.

'Am I the only person in this house capable of hearing the doorbell?' Elizabeth yelled as she walked through the hall, wiping her hands on the apron.

The woman standing on the other side of the screen-door wore an apologetic smile. Elizabeth knew at once that the woman had heard her complaint. A sales-woman, and probably a determined one. A girl of about Julia's age stood half-hidden by the woman—along to win the hearts of her grandmother's prospective customers, no doubt. Elizabeth gave the woman a polite smile of enquiry.

'I should have called first, I know,' the woman said immediately. 'But I didn't want to make too much of my stopping by.' Elizabeth's confusion must have communicated itself to the woman for she uttered a self-deprecating laugh before adding, 'It would help, I expect, if I introduced myself. I'm Hannah Harcourt. And this,' she nodded towards the child, 'is Linda, Andrew's daughter.'

Elizabeth wondered if she looked as stunned as she felt. 'Hannah Harcourt,' she repeated. 'Andrew's wife?'

'No, no, my dear. Andrew's mother. But thank you for the compliment. Andrew isn't married.'

'But you just said...'

Mrs Harcourt's blue eyes twinkled. 'I know. Confusing, isn't it? May I come in? I should have called first,' she repeated, 'but...'

At a loss for words, Elizabeth stood aside so that the pair could enter. After one quick glance at Andrew's mother, her gaze was riveted on his daughter. About the same size as Julia, she was all arms and legs, her flyaway hair lighter in colour than Andrew's, though she had the same intensely blue eyes and dark eyebrows. Directed by her grandmother to speak to Elizabeth, the young girl mumbled something to the floor. Painfully shy, Elizabeth decided.

'It looks as if I'm interrupting some baking.' Only Mrs Harcourt seemed to be at ease.

Elizabeth looked down at her apron. A large smear of chocolate decorated the front. 'Yes, I'm sorry. I'm making pies. Do you mind visiting in the kitchen?'

'Not at all,' Mrs Harcourt assured her, following Elizabeth down the hall.

The kitchen was redolent with the scent of spices and chocolate. Julia turned from her perch in front of the stove. 'I didn't stop stirring one second. Hello.' The latter was addressed to the two following Elizabeth.

'Thank you, sweetheart. This is Mrs Harcourt and Linda. My sister Julia. Maybe you two would like to go up to Julia's room and play.'

With a joyful whoop Julia grabbed Linda's hand and dragged the reluctant girl from the room. Mrs Harcourt looked a little anxious.

'She'll be OK,' Elizabeth said. 'What Julia lacks in good manners, she makes up for in kindness.'

'It's not easy at my age to be suddenly presented with a little girl,' Mrs Harcourt admitted.

Elizabeth carefully poured the chocolate filling into the prepared crusts. A daughter. Andrew had a daughter.

'I came to thank you. Andrew is so dear to my husband and me. He's an only child. I lost two babies before him, and then I had so much trouble delivering Andrew that the doctor decreed no more. Poor Andrew. He was so cosseted and coddled it's a wonder he didn't die of suffocation. I watched over him and protected him and literally planned his every move, his every breath. Of course, he rebelled. Always having to prove that he was tougher and stronger than the other boys. Sometimes I think that he went into the oil business just so that he could get out from under the burden of our caring so much.' She smiled her thanks as Elizabeth handed her a glass of lemonade. 'Unfortunately he fell in love with a girl who was as cosseted and coddled as he had been. He thought that they were kindred spirits, but they weren't. The marriage never took place.' She sipped from her glass. 'She finally married this spring, so Linda is out here to spend the summer with her father. She'd never met him before, so you can imagine the difficulties.'

'Poor little girl,' Elizabeth said instinctively.

'She misses her mother and her friends. She's lonely and she's bored.' Friendly blue eyes smiled across the table at Elizabeth. 'From what little Andrew divulged about his visit here last week, boredom is not a problem in your house. What did happen, anyway? He was a sight.'

'I hope his clothes weren't ruined.' At the negative shake of Mrs Harcourt's head, Elizabeth described the occurrences of the other day. At first she was hesitant and apologetic, but as the story progressed it became clear that Andrew's mother relished his mishaps as thoroughly as had Elizabeth.

'My dear,' Mrs Harcourt said, wiping her tearing eyes, 'how in the world did you ever keep from laughing?'

'I'm afraid that I didn't, Mrs Harcourt. The look on Andrew's face when he saw Barney...' Mirth clogged her voice.

'Please, call me Hannah. I wish I could have been there.' Andrew's mother chortled with laughter. 'Now that it's much too late, I see that I erred in bringing Andrew up in such a structured atmosphere. It's hardly fair of me to wish at this late date that he was a little less rigid in the way that he lives his life.' From upstairs came a loud thumping sound, followed by footsteps racing down the staircase. Hannah looked enquiringly at Elizabeth. 'Eight children, I believe Andrew said.'

Before Elizabeth could answer, Tommy came flying into the kitchen, Abigail in hot pursuit. 'Give me back my diary!'

'Watch out!' Elizabeth cried.

Too late—Tommy, sliding into a turn, slid too far. Two chocolate pies flew through the air to land face down at Elizabeth's feet.

'Thomas Kennedy Asher, you clean up this mess right now and then you fix something for tonight's dessert. And it had better be edible.' Elizabeth didn't raise her voice, but Tommy recognised the implacable tone.

Bending over, he threw his arms around her. 'Sorry, Elizabeth, I'll take care of it.'

Hannah stood up. 'I think it's time for Linda and me to leave.'

Five minutes earlier would have been better, Elizabeth thought bitterly as she went to fetch the small girl. Then Hannah would have been spared another rendition of the Asher family at its worst. Linda left with great reluctance after a long and drawn-out parting scene with Julia. Apparently the girls had become bosom buddies in their short period of acquaintance. Elizabeth hoped that Julia wasn't cherishing any fond hopes of renewing that acquaintance. After Hannah went home and described her visit to Andrew, that should take care of any of the Ashers ever seeing any of the Harcourts again.

'Elizabeth, how can you bear to live with us?' Tommy came up silently behind her and draped his arm over her shoulder.

'How could I bear not to?' she rejoined, reaching up to tousle his dark hair.

'I'd miss you all,' she said to Mai Tai the next evening, as the cat sat curled up in her lap. They were alone in the living-room. The older children were out, the middle ones watching television in the basement and the youngest all asleep. Her mother was in the studio, totally immersed in her latest project. Even the dogs were quiet. The Harcourts, mother and son, would never believe it if they saw how peaceful the house is now, she thought. Not that she cared if the Harcourts disapproved of the Asher lifestyle. At least her home was filled with love and laughter. Milk would sour around Andrew Harcourt. An only child, undoubtedly used to having his own way. She pitied his little girl. First her father had abandoned her mother before her birth, and now her mother had abandoned her in favour of a new husband. Poor unwanted child, mailed off to a father who'd never bothered to see her. Andrew Harcourt hadn't struck her as a man who would evade his responsibilities.

Which proved that it was impossible to judge a man's character by his lovemaking. If she had met Andrew in the normal course of her life she probably wouldn't have given him a second thought. Tall, strong men who believed in silent suffering did nothing to elevate her blood-pressure. Even less did she admire men who lacked a sense of humour. Andrew's weakness, his vulnerability, was what had appealed to her. He'd needed her.

And at the charity ball? The night and the music, she told herself. And the little-boy-lost look in his eyes when he'd struggled with his memory. His snap judgement of her was so far off the mark that it would have been laughable if she hadn't been so angry with him, not only for daring to make it, but for having the utter gall to say it to her face. 'Well, he's no coward,' she grudgingly admitted to Mai Tai. Andrew liked her even less than she liked him. In spite of his kisses, he'd made it quite clear that the further he was away from Elizabeth Asher, the better he liked it.

The phone rang sharply at her elbow and she jumped, dislodging the large cat. Mai Tai gave a delicate shake to her ruffled fur before leaving the room, her tail waving indignantly behind her.

'May I speak with Elizabeth, please.'

She gripped the receiver tightly in her hand. Had she conjured him up with her thoughts? 'Speaking.'

There was a slight pause, and then Andrew's voice was cool and distant in her ear as he explained the purpose of his call. Hannah and Linda had both been full of their visit the previous afternoon—she could imagine—and he had a tremendous favour to ask of her. His strong reluctance to do so surged over the line. He spoke at great length about Linda's loneliness—making no mention of the fact that his daughter was a stranger to him through his own choosing—and spoke of the difficulties of entertaining her. Elizabeth might have been more sympathetic with his problems if she hadn't sensed that he was rambling on to avoid coming to the purpose of his call. Obviously the very thought of asking Elizabeth Asher for a favour was about to choke him. Finally, he said that his mother had come up with a suggestion. His tone of voice implied that the whole idea was ridiculous and that he was only calling to appease his mother and, furthermore, that he had no difficulty in believing that Elizabeth would instantly refuse. At this point Andrew's voice grew so hopeful that Elizabeth had difficulty restraining herself from breaking into laughter. Only curiosity kept her silent. What was it that he wanted?

'And so, Mother thought—that is, I wondered if you could take Linda off her hands during the day?'

Elizabeth was glad that no one was there to see the way her jaw dropped. 'I couldn't possibly.' Her heart bled for the poor child. Shunted from pillar to post, always in someone's way. Hannah Harcourt had seemed so nice—how could she possibly say that she wanted her granddaughter taken off her hands?

'I didn't think you would.' His voice almost purred with satisfaction.

The sound immediately aroused Elizabeth's fighting instincts. 'Unless, of course,' she purred back, 'you meant for her to come to our house. We'd be delighted to have her spend her days with us.' There. She stuck her tongue out at the receiver. Let's see him get out of that one.

'How much do you charge?'

Charge! Red spots flared in front of her eyes before she realised what he was doing. Try to make her back down, would he? She ran quick figures through her mind. What was high enough to really stick it to him, and yet, at the same time, reasonable enough so that he wouldn't guess what she was doing? Stalling for time, she asked, 'Would you prefer to pay by the week or the day?'

'Day,' he spat.

Temper, temper, Mr Harcourt. Elizabeth could hardly stifle her own laughter. Hoist with his own petard, was Andrew T. Harcourt. She paid her cleaning ladies six dollars an hour. Say, a seven-hour day...thirty-five dollars...no, that had to be way too much. The sound of his breathing registered his impatience. 'Thirty-five dollars a day.'

'Fine. We'll see you at seven in the morning.' He hung up before she could reply.

Mai Tai leaped gracefully back on to her lap. Elizabeth absent-mindedly scratched behind the cat's pointed ears. 'He thinks he got in the last word. We'll see.' Her mouth twitched as she thought back over their conversation. 'He hated it, Mai Tai, you have no idea how much he hated it.' The cat twisted up her head and miaowed. 'You're absolutely right. Why did he call and ask me, if he hated it so much? Definitely food for thought. Mr Andrew T. Harcourt may have more to him than I've suspected.' She cradled the cat's head between her hands and gave it a little shake. 'And if you know what's good for you, young lady, you will inform your friends to stay out of his way. No matter what Andrew T. Harcourt thinks of us, that little girl needs us. I don't want anything to happen that will change his mind about leaving her with us.' She settled back in her chair to think about the small girl. Unfortunately it was Linda's father who succeeded in snaring the majority of her thoughts.

CHAPTER THREE

ELIZABETH was ready at six-thirty the next morning, just in case Andrew arrived early in the hope of catching her unprepared. The house was in order, the appetising smell of coffee drifted down the hallway, the family was quietly sleeping and the animals were locked in the basement. As for herself, she hadn't forgotten Andrew's charge that she was irresponsible and frivolous, and she had dressed specifically to erase that image. Blonde hair was neatly braided into a chignon while the plain old shirtwaister dress she'd dug up from the back of her closet would give Anna Belle hives if she saw it. However, it lent Elizabeth's trim body an air of practicality and competence. It was too hot to wear stockings, but her bare legs rose from sturdy, serviceable canvas shoes. One look at her and Andrew would know that he need have no qualms about leaving his daughter with her.

How annoying, therefore, that Andrew barely acknowledged her presence with a grumpy greeting before striding away. No kiss for Linda; merely a curt admonition to behave. Even the way he ground the gears of his car demonstrated his total lack of charity with the situation. Elizabeth stood in the doorway of the screened front porch and wished with all her heart that she had a hose in her hands. If ever a man needed humanising...

A small sound at her side dragged her attention away from the dark car speeding down the street.

47

Linda was scuffing her toe against the porch floor. Elizabeth could feel the waves of apprehension flowing from the small girl. All thoughts of Andrew fled. Linda might have a father lacking in the basic skills when it came to manners and fatherhood, but that didn't mean that she couldn't have friends who'd teach her about love and laughter. Elizabeth held out her hand. 'I think it's time we rescued the animals from the basement and woke up Julia.'

By five o'clock, when Andrew returned for Linda, Elizabeth would have judged the day to be a total success. If Andrew had asked her. Which he most emphatically did not.

'What the hell are you doing?'

Andrew's shout was Elizabeth's first warning of his arrival. She looked down from her high perch. Andrew's face glared up through the leaves. 'I'm teaching Linda the proper way to climb trees. Do you realise that this child has never been in a tree before?'

'Are you some kind of lunatic? Linda, you get down here right this instant.' His voice softened. 'Don't worry, I'll catch you if you fall.'

'She's not going to fall,' Elizabeth said indignantly. 'Just remember what I showed you, Linda. Tummy to the trunk and always have one hand holding firmly before you let go with the other, and test each branch with your foot before you put your weight on it.' She watched triumphantly as the small girl scrambled successfully down the tree. When the glowing face turned upwards for her approval, Elizabeth was swift to give it. 'Wonderful!'

'Wonderful? She could have broken her neck!'

'I know. I found her up in this tree absolutely terrified because she had no idea how to get down. It's a miracle that she didn't panic and jump. Now she can climb like a monkey.'

'Linda, go and collect your things.' As the child departed Andrew raised his head. 'I don't suppose that it ever occurred to you to simply get out a stepladder, help her down and then forbid her to ever climb a tree again,' he spat through clenched teeth.

Elizabeth stared down at him. 'Andrew, you can't be serious! If you have a tree and a child it's impossible to keep them apart. Unless you chop down the tree. The only sensible thing to do is to teach the child to climb safely.'

Green leaves framed Andrew's face, highlighting his struggle to control his temper. He was only partially successful. 'Get down here,' he snapped. 'I want to talk to you and I do not intend to strain my neck doing it.'

Who did that man think he was? Bossing her around—he could... A memory of Linda's woebegone face flashed before her eyes. For Linda's sake she would appease her father. 'All right, I'm coming down,' she said. Outward appearances to the contrary, she was seething. Rapidly descending from branch to branch, absorbed in silently enumerating Andrew's multitude of sins, Elizabeth failed to follow her own advice to Linda. Rashly, she put her full weight on a branch that she'd neglected to test. Too late she realised that the early spring winds must have weakened the limb. With a loud crack the wood splintered and both Elizabeth and the limb plummeted to the ground.

Andrew grabbed for her but his injured arm was no match for the velocity of her fall, and they tumbled to the ground. Andrew lay beneath her on the grass, a pained expression on his face. His eyes were closed.

Elizabeth's gaze flew to his injured shoulder. 'Are you OK?' she asked anxiously.

'I will be as soon as you get off my stomach.'

'Oh. Sorry.' She rolled off and propped herself up on one elbow. Andrew's eyes remained closed. 'Are you sure you're all right?'

'What have I ever done to you?' he asked.

'Andrew, I'm sorry. I've been up and down that tree so many times I can climb it in my sleep.'

'Maybe you should have. Then I wouldn't be here.'

He still didn't open his eyes. What if he had another concussion? Bumping his head so soon after the last time. Elizabeth leaned over his chest. 'Open your eyes.'

'Why?'

'So that I can see your pupils. You might have another concussion.'

'I don't.'

'Then why won't you open your eyes?'

'If I do, will you have disappeared?' He opened his eyes. 'So much for wishes.'

Ignoring his whimsical remarks, Elizabeth carefully studied his pupils, her face inches from his. 'I don't see any sign of concussion.'

The blue in his eyes darkened with some emotion. 'You have a scratch on your face. It's bleeding.' He took a handkerchief from his pocket and wiped her cheek.

'I can get it.' She tried to sit up.

Andrew's arm around her waist was immovable. 'Lie still. I've almost got it.' He dabbed gently at her skin. 'You drive me crazy. You know that, don't you?'

'Andrew, I——'

'No, don't say anything.' He rubbed his thumb over her full bottom lip. 'Dreamy blue eyes, so innocent-looking. Your hair, tangled and wild, but shining like a halo in the sun. Skin that's almost translucent. Ethereal. You look like an angel, but you're no angel, are you, Elizabeth?' The arm around her waist tightened. 'You're flesh and blood.' A hand in her hair pulled her face down to his. 'Damn you for haunting my dreams,' he muttered against her mouth.

The warmth of the afternoon sun on Elizabeth's back was feeble compared to the heat that flooded through her veins at the touch of Andrew's lips. She was dimly aware of muted traffic noises, of children's voices on the other side of the house, of a humming-bird whistling past en route to the geraniums . . . and then all those sounds faded away, to be replaced by the whisper of Andrew's breathing, the pounding of his heart. Tommy had worked in the garden earlier and the sweet smell of freshly mown grass mingled with Andrew's masculine scent.

After one deep kiss that melted her bones, enabling him to mould her body to fit the angles of his, Andrew contented himself with little nibbling kisses on her lips that teased and excited Elizabeth. When she could no longer endure this exquisite torment she cupped her hands around his face, holding his head immobile while she explored his mouth with a boldness that shocked her even as it pleasured her.

'Definitely no angel,' Andrew murmured, his breath mingling with hers. He traced the curvature of her spine from neck to waist, and then his hand travelled slowly over her hip until his fingers trailed along the bottom of her shorts, his touch igniting a fiery path

along her bare skin. His other hand found its way
inside her cotton T-shirt and she shivered with pleasure
as he found her swelling breast unencumbered by a
bra. Pleasure turned to need as he rolled the sensitive
tip between two fingers. With a quick shift of his
muscles Andrew rolled over, so that Elizabeth lay half
beneath him and half beside him. His legs were entangled with hers but their upper bodies didn't touch
as he leaned over her, shading her from the sun.

She opened her eyes. The heavy-lidded look of
passion was fading from his face, to be replaced by
a baffled expression. 'This is hardly the time or the
place.'

Weakly she shook her head. Let him take it for
agreement. How else could she respond to a remark
like that? Was she supposed to make an appointment
with him so that he could take her to bed and banish
once and for all this hated attraction that she sup-
posedly held for him? There would never be the time
or place for that. She wasn't a disease that he could
inoculate himself against with one exposure. She
opened her mouth to tell him so.

'What the hell——?' Andrew exploded, leaping to
his feet.

With an incredible sense of atrocious timing the
automatic sprinkler system had switched on. Elizabeth
gasped with shock as cold water rained down upon
her, and thankfully grabbed the hand that Andrew
extended. She could feel the laughter bubbling to the
surface as they ran through a rainbow created by the
sun shining on the spray.

Andrew was not amused, as was clearly evident by
the black thundercloud on the face that turned to her

once they'd reached the dry safety of the front garden. 'I might have known that you'd be amused.'

'We must have looked awfully silly.'

'Everything is a big joke to you. How you can stand here and ignore the fact that we came damned near to making a spectacle of ourselves back there, not to mention the fact that this suit is probably ruined and——'

'May I remind you that it wasn't my idea to engage in a spot of lovemaking on the back lawn.' She was darned if she would apologise. 'Nor was it my fault that the sprinklers happened to turn on. I'm sorry about your suit but if you send it to a decent cleaners they could take care of it.' Fists jammed on hips she glared at him, her head flung back defiantly.

Having stated her case so eloquently, she was more than a little taken aback when, instead of contritely begging her forgiveness, Andrew leered at the front of her T-shirt.

'While in your family it may be perfectly acceptable to run around looking as if you're auditioning for a wet T-shirt contest, I'd prefer it if you'd show a little more modesty around my daughter.'

Elizabeth's gaze dropped to her chest. Her T-shirt was wetter than she'd realised and the thin knit clung to her body, clearly delineating two hard, thrusting nipples. Hastily she crossed her arms over her breasts.

Andrew uttered a lewd chuckle. 'That little spot of lovemaking, as you call it, may not have been your idea, but I sure didn't notice you fighting me off.'

'You might have had another head injury. I didn't want to cause any further damage.'

Thankfully, before he could expose that excuse for the nonsense it was, Julia and Linda came tearing from the house.

'You're all wet,' Julia said.

At the same time, Linda chirped, 'Sorry it took me so long. I was waiting for the clothes-drier to finish.'

Andrew gave Elizabeth a look loaded with sarcasm before asking his daughter why her clothes were wet.

'I was changing Hewie's diaper, and I took off the wet one and didn't put anything over his...you know.' She put her hand over her mouth and giggled. 'Paige says that he does that whenever the cold air hits it.'

Her hand caught his attention. 'What's the bandage for?'

'I burned myself. Julia and I were fixing some grilled cheese sandwiches and——'

'You allowed these children to use the stove?' He pinned an accusing glare on Elizabeth.

'They have to learn. It's only a little burn. And she'll be more careful next time. The only reason she's wearing a bandage is because I wanted her to keep it clean while she was playing outside.'

'Climbing trees,' Andrew added coldly.

'Well, yes.'

'What else did you do today, Linda? Play chicken in the street with cars, learn to make dynamite, perhaps chop wood with a rusty hatchet?'

Elizabeth saw the look of confusion on the faces of the two girls. They didn't totally understand what was happening, but they did recognise that Andrew was angry. They simply weren't sure who was in trouble.

'It's all right, Linda. Your father isn't mad at you. He's just a little unhappy because he got caught in the sprinkler,' Elizabeth explained. 'Tell Julia goodbye and run along.'

At least Andrew had the grace to look slightly ashamed. Forcing a smile to his face, he said, 'Wait in the car. I want to speak to Elizabeth.'

'All right.' Linda turned to Elizabeth. 'I had a wonderful time. Thank you.'

Elizabeth bent down and gave the small girl a big hug. 'We had a wonderful time, too.'

Linda giggled. 'You're all wet and cold.' She returned Elizabeth's embrace and then the two children ran laughing to the car, where Linda dutifully got into the front seat.

Elizabeth turned back to Andrew. She knew what he was going to say, but she had no intention of making it easier for him.

'I'll be making other arrangements for Linda in the future,' he said. 'I'm afraid that this isn't working out.'

'For whom? For Linda?'

'Linda isn't old enough to know what's best for her.'

'What did you have in mind? A padded cell? Sure, she'll get her share of bruises and bumps over here. That's part of growing up. But she also receives respect and liking and love and laughter. Something that you, Mr Andrew T. Harcourt, know absolutely nothing about.'

A sanctimonious smile distorted his mouth and he leaned closer to her. 'I love the way your nipples stick out when you're angry.'

Intent on convincing him of Linda's needs, Elizabeth had totally forgotten about her wet T-shirt. By the time she'd recovered her composure he was getting into his car. As the engine roared into life she could hear Linda yelling good bye. She only imagined that she could hear Andrew fiendishly laughing. A slow smile curved her lips. Linda might be painfully shy, but she had turned out to be a child who knew her own mind. Andrew was fooling himself if he thought that he'd had the last word.

It was almost eleven. Elizabeth was about to give up. Andrew must be holding out longer than she'd anticipated. 'Unless he's merely putting off a task he's very reluctant to do,' she said to the white pile of fluff in her lap. Coconut the cat yawned her uninterest.

The phone rang sharply. Elizabeth picked it up after the first ring.

'Expecting my call?' Andrew asked drily.

'I thought that perhaps you didn't know how determined a child Linda is,' she carefully explained.

He snorted. 'Manipulative is the word you want, isn't it?'

'I don't know. Tell me what happened.'

'She listened to all my reasoning and seemed to be perfectly willing to abide by my decision. Then for the rest of the evening she maintained a delicate balance between two emotions: listless despair that I was ruining her life, and total enthusiasm when she thought of some other wonderful thing that Elizabeth had introduced her to today. Yes, I knew you'd think it was funny.'

He didn't sound terribly annoyed. None the less, Elizabeth controlled her amusement. There was no sense beating a man when he was down. 'Does this mean that we'll be seeing Linda tomorrow?'

'Don't be so damned coy. You knew all along that she'd be back.'

'I wasn't sure how strong your opposition was.'

'Not strong enough to fight my mother, too.'

'Your mother?' Elizabeth asked in surprise.

'She called Linda to ask how the day had gone. By the time I was called to the phone, I never stood a chance.'

Elizabeth swallowed her laughter. 'Well, thank you for calling,' she said formally. 'We'll look forward to seeing you tomorrow.'

'Elizabeth, one quick question . . . Were you aware that a window in Julia's room overlooks the back garden?' He hung up before she could reply.

Darn that man and his ability to get in the last word. And what had that cryptic question about Julia's window been all about? Her veins flooded with embarrassment. The girls had seen her and Andrew on the grass. That explained all the sly looks Julia had been giving her during dinner tonight. Those two little minxes. She wondered how Andrew had found out, and how he'd explained the situation to his daughter. If he could tease Elizabeth about it . . . maybe there was hope for him after all.

For the next few days Elizabeth kept a close eye on the two girls. Andrew might have reversed his decision, but she never doubted that his change of heart had been made reluctantly. It wouldn't take much for him to change his mind again if he truly believed that Linda would be safer elsewhere. Fortunately for his peace of mind and her efforts, Laura had come up with the grand scheme of writing and performing a play for the family, and since her plans encompassed Julia and Linda as well as Susan the four of them spent most of their hours busily and safely ensconced in Laura's room.

Encounters between Elizabeth and Andrew were casual and kept to a minimum. Obviously Andrew had no intention of risking a repeat of the other afternoon. Which was fine with Elizabeth. Her only goal was to shake Andrew up a little, jiggle his funny-bone, make him less serious and a little more tolerant of human behaviour and frailty. Even his mother conceded that he was a little on the rigid side. Certainly Elizabeth had no thought of any kind of relationship with Andrew. There was no room in her life for a man.

That her life was unconventional she already knew. It suited her, and that was the important thing. She should have known that Andrew wouldn't approve. He startled her one afternoon by accepting her offer of a glass of lemonade. They sat in the protected shade of the screened front porch, Elizabeth in the wooden swing and Andrew in a nearby wicker chair.

He brought up the subject of her parents. 'It's strange that I've never seen them when I'm picking up or delivering Linda.'

'Not so strange. Max has a townhouse over by the Broadmoor. He and my mother decided long ago that they couldn't live together but neither could they live apart, so she lives here and he lives there, and they sort of, well, get together by pre-arrangement. It's not for everyone, but eight children seem to indicate that it works for them.' She pushed the swing into motion with her foot.

'That would be Max Asher, the developer. And your mother is Anna Belle, the artist.'

'How did you know that?'

'I did a background check on you.'

'You did what?' Elizabeth stopped swinging and looked at him in surprise.

'I wasn't about to entrust my daughter to strangers without knowing something about them.'

'I trust you were satisfied.'

'Linda's here, isn't she?'

'I'm curious. What did you learn?'

'Your father has an impeccable business reputation, even if his lifestyle is considered a little liberated. Everyone assumes that that's his wife's influence. Your mother is very respected in the art world and is seen occasionally on the social scene. Less charitable people grumble that it's easy to be a success when one is married to a wealthy, influential man and never has to worry about the hazards of day-to-day living. Several mentioned how fortunate she was to have you to shoulder the responsibilities of motherhood for her.'

Elizabeth gave a peal of laughter. 'They think that Anna Belle takes advantage of me?'

'Cleaning this enormous old house, caring for and feeding nine, no, twelve of you, while she does her own thing.'

'It's not like that at all,' Elizabeth rejoined. 'In the first place, cleaning ladies come in four mornings a week and they do most of the laundry, too. All of us cook, although I admit that I do most of that. I pay all the bills, keep everyone clothed, see that everyone gets to dentists and doctors, keep track of everyone's schedules, take care of household correspondence . . . What I really am is a glorified manager. We used to go through housekeepers the way other people go through paper tissues. When I graduated from high school, I didn't have any particular career in mind and going to college simply to go seemed a little silly. We'd just lost our third housekeeper in so many months, so I went to Max and asked him what he paid housekeepers. When he told me, I crossed my fingers behind my back and said that if he'd pay me double that, I'd take the job until I decided what I wanted to do with my life. It was all a joke to him, but he hadn't been able to find a replacement and thought that he had nothing to lose by letting me take over, at least for the summer. After six months he gave me a rise and we've all been dealing famously together since then.'

'What about marriage, your own family?'

Elizabeth shrugged. 'Haven't missed them so far.'

'No wonder, with the example set by your parents.'

Swallowing the temptation to argue, Elizabeth said, 'Tell me about your parents.'

'They're both high school teachers. At least, Mom still is. Dad's a principal. I grew up over in Gunnison, Colorado. Mom quit teaching to have me and didn't go back until a few years ago when they moved over here so that Dad could take the principal's job.' He added firmly, 'I don't believe in working mothers.'

Elizabeth sipped her lemonade. 'Be careful that Anna Belle doesn't hear you say that. She's a staunch feminist.'

'With a name like Anna Belle?'

'She calls it her cross.' Elizabeth laughed. 'Haven't you noticed our names?'

He glanced across the porch at her. 'Elizabeth sounds like a very feminine, old-fashioned name.'

'It's also the name of English queens, the mother of John the Baptist, Elizabeth Barrett Browning, the poet who defied her father for love of a man, Elizabeth Stanton, a suffragette, Elizabeth Blackwell, the first woman doctor in America and last, but not least, Elizabeth Bennet, the spirited heroine of *Pride and Prejudice.*'

'Good lord,' he declared.

Elizabeth set the swing in motion again. 'Now it's your turn. What's the "T" stand for?'

'No one forced you to explain your name.'

'Meaning you won't tell me. I can't believe how sensitive you are about a silly name.'

'I never hear anyone in your family call you Liz or Lizzie.'

'And they had better not if they want to live.'

Andrew shook his head. 'I can't believe you're so sensitive about a silly name.'

'*Touché.* I won't mention it again. Unless provoked.'

'Meaning?'

'When you get so unbearably stuffy that I can't stand it.'

He set his glass down and stood up. 'You go out of your way to try and irritate me, don't you?'

'Not very far. You're so easy to irritate.'

'Why me? What do you have against me? Do you resent having had to rescue me, is that it?'

'Don't be silly. I merely think that you're a little too serious. You need your tail-feathers ruffled every now and again. It's good for you.'

He grabbed the chains of the swing and held it motionless. Leaning down, he brought his face close to hers. 'And you, Elizabeth,' he growled in a low voice, 'should have your tail-feathers paddled. And more than now and again.'

The porch door slammed behind him. Of all the nerve, she thought indignantly. A second thought immediately supplanted her indignation and she jumped to her feet and hurried after him.

She found him in the back garden chatting with Abigail. At least, Abigail was chatting. Andrew appeared to be chafing at the bit to get away. No wonder. Elizabeth grinned to herself as she heard the topic of conversation. Andrew's interest in the various shades of nail-polish that Abigail was experimenting with was doubtlessly nil. She could hardly wait until Linda reached that age—which reminded her of why she was chasing him. 'Where's Linda?'

The relief on his face at her question was pathetic. 'She forgot something inside. Did you want to talk to me?'

His expression was so hopeful that she almost said no, but this was too important. She led him out of range of Abigail's hearing. 'Earlier, on the porch.' Darn. This was going to be more difficult than she'd imagined. 'You spoke of paddling...'

'Don't tell me that it appealed to you as much as it appealed to me?' he mocked.

'Andrew, I'm serious. This is important. I want to know what you really think of spanking.'

'I have to admit that it's a—er—pastime that I have never indulged in, but——'

'Be serious. I'm talking about Linda.'

Her words wiped the smirk from his face. His eyes narrowed ominously. 'Go on.'

'There isn't any "go on". I mean, some people believe that spanking children is OK and——'

'Am I to assume that you found it necessary to spank Linda today?'

'Of course not. I don't believe in physical punishment. It doesn't teach the child anything but to be afraid of the person, usually bigger, who hit him.'

'Then I'm afraid that I don't understand what you're getting at.'

'You,' she said desperately. 'When you said paddling, it made me wonder if you...' She quailed before his anger.

'Damn you. Are you asking me if I plan to beat my daughter?'

'No! It's just that, I know you don't know anything about raising kids, and I was worried that you might lose your patience, because after all she is only a child and can't be expected to always behave the way you want her to and I know you think it's a big bother having her out here now when you've never cared anything about her and——'

'What the hell are you talking about?' He backed her up against the side of the house.

She didn't think she'd ever before seen a person so angry, but she refused to back down. 'Your mother told me. How you'd abandoned your girlfriend when she was pregnant and how you'd never seen Linda before this summer.'

'My mother never told you any such lies.' His voice was as cold as a March blizzard.

'Andrew, it's as obvious as the nose on your face that you and Linda are total strangers to each other.'

'And, therefore, that's my fault, is that what you're saying?'

'Well, isn't it?'

'The hell with you, Miss Asher. I don't need to explain anything to you. And don't look for Linda tomorrow. She won't be back.'

When she would have reached out to stop him he slapped her hand out of his way and strode off to his car, where he sat until Linda ran from the house to join him. The low-riding sun silhouetted his face. Angry, forbidding, it looked carved in stone. Elizabeth slumped to the ground as Andrew drove away, her shaking legs refusing to support her any longer. There was nothing she could do or say to set back the clock. And why should she want to? Even if she'd known how angry her words would make him, she'd have had to say them. She couldn't bear it if Andrew hit his daughter. Although why she thought he would, just because of a teasing remark . . . if only Andrew hadn't been the type of man who'd abandoned his fiancée; if only he hadn't abandoned Linda. How could a man refuse to acknowledge a child born of his passion, a child that sprang from his own loins, a child that carried his genes, his blue eyes, his wiry frame? Elizabeth buried her head in her arms on her knees and wept. She didn't know if the tears were for Linda, for Andrew or for herself.

When the phone rang an hour later Elizabeth didn't bother to answer it. At this time of the day the phone was constantly ringing for Abigail, Tommy or Georgia.

'Elizabeth!' Georgia shouted down the staircase. 'That was Andrew Harcourt on the phone and he said that he would be by in twenty minutes to pick you up and you damned well better be ready to go and don't yell at me for swearing because I am quoting his exact words.'

Even with five bathrooms, when ten people—all but two female—shared them, all the members of the family had of necessity, learned speed and economy in the bathroom. Elizabeth was showered, dressed and sitting in the porch swing when Andrew drove up. As a gesture of friendship she was wearing the blouse he'd given her to replace the one she'd ripped up. A pretty floral skirt and white sandals completed her outfit. Her hair, still slightly damp, hung loose around her shoulders. Not wanting Andrew to think that she considered this a date, she was wearing the barest minimum of make-up with only a touch of pale pink on her lips.

He stepped from the car, but when he saw her sitting there he halted and gestured impatiently for her to join him. His mood had obviously not improved since he'd left this afternoon. With an inward sigh, Elizabeth went down the drive. He held the car door for her, barely allowing her to settle in place before he slammed it shut. She took one peep at his stormy face and then concentrated on fastening her seatbelt. Andrew had called this meeting to order; it was up to him to begin.

The sun had not yet set as Andrew edged from the driveway of their large, three-storey Victorian house on to Cascade Avenue. Crimson roses trailing over the ornate wrought-iron fence perfumed the air through Elizabeth's open car window. A neighbour was watering his evergreen trees, the new growth spring-green against the older, darker needles. Robins and starlings danced in the spray of another neighbour's sprinklers before being startled into flight by passing joggers.

Andrew drove as if he had a destination in mind. Elizabeth didn't ask. He could hardly be kidnapping her, since her entire family knew that she was out with him. Finally the silence grew unbearable. 'Do you like your new car?' she asked. She knew that the one stolen by his muggers had been abandoned down by San Luis.

'Yes. I couldn't have driven the other one even if those hoods hadn't wrecked it.' He glanced in her direction. 'I was luckier than the couple who stopped to help them.'

'I saw it in the paper. The wife died immediately, the man later in hospital. He couldn't understand; said he told them to take the car the minute they showed their guns. How can people be so violent?' Ouch. That was uncomfortably close to their topic of conversation this afternoon. They were passing the old Van Briggle pottery building and, anxious to change the subject, she quickly pointed out the garden club plots behind. 'Look at the beautiful iris. I've never seen such gorgeous colours.'

Andrew gave her a sardonic look. He'd followed her thoughts with uncanny accuracy. 'Don't I recognise that blouse?' When she nodded, he asked, 'Is wearing it a deliberate choice on your part to remind me that I'm in your debt?' He swung the car into a parking area adjacent to Monument Valley Park.

'No, of course not. How could you think such a thing?'

'How could you think that I'd beat a child?'

'I never accused you of any such thing. Besides . . .' She fell silent.

'Besides?'

'She is only a child. No matter what you thought, I had to say what I was thinking. I'm sorry if I hurt your feelings, but you must see that Linda is more important than that. I mean, we all have to protect those unable to protect themselves. Even if the results are sometimes—well, uncomfortable.'

'Have you ever had any reason to suspect that I would actually strike a child?'

'No, of course not. Even when you said that, about paddling, I know you were teasing, but——'

'I'm not so sure,' he said grimly, getting out of the car and coming round to open her door.

She ignored the implied threat. 'It's just that—I'm sorry Andrew, but I simply can't understand a father who would callously abandon a child.'

They walked along the dirt-path bordering the deep-banked river. Birds chirped loudly above the traffic sounds which flowed from the nearby interstate highway. Cotton from the cottonwood trees lined the path in white. A Brewer's blackbird took to the air at their approach, his body distinctive with the greenish sheen of the black feathers.

'That's what it all comes down to, isn't it. My abandoning her before she was born.'

'Yes.' Misery settled over her like a descending cloak.

A slow-moving train passed noisily along the edge of the park. To the west the setting sun dramatically outlined the clouds above Pikes Peak with yellow. Nearer to hand, tennis balls pounded on the park's courts, each thud deepening Elizabeth's depression. Why didn't Andrew say something?

'I was furious when I left you this afternoon. You were obviously convinced of my guilt, yet I knew that my mother couldn't have told you that I'd behaved so badly,' he said. 'At first I tried to convince myself that you were lying, but I couldn't come up with any reason why you would.'

Her spirits sank even lower. She'd been hoping that Andrew was going to come up with an excuse for his behaviour that would absolve him, at least partially, of all blame. Instead, he was going to deny everything. She shook her head, as if to ward off his lies. 'I can see, anyone can see, that you and Linda behave as total strangers towards each other.'

'Because we are, dammit. Would you please just listen with an open mind? I called my mother and asked her about your conversation. It wasn't until then that she realised that she'd left out a few pertinent points in blabbing my life history.'

'She meant well.'

'That's what Benedict Arnold and Kim Philby claimed.'

'Andrew! You can't compare your mother to——'

'No, I know.' He ran his fingers wildly through his hair. 'It's been a damned unsettling day.'

CHAPTER FOUR

'Growing up, I wasn't allowed to play sports. Mom was afraid that I'd get hurt. Getting into cars with teenage drivers was absolutely forbidden. I didn't get my own licence until a year after I was eligible. Needless to say, I never climbed trees.'

In the growing dusk, she felt him glance down at her.

'Raised the way I was, it's instinctive with me to want to protect Linda from the world, even though I know that it's the wrong way to bring up a child. My parents didn't intend to make me feel that I was different from the other boys, but I did. I felt like a weakling. I used to fantasise that I'd run away and join the French Foreign Legion. Instead I went off to college. Freedom went to my head. I almost flunked out the first year. That frightened me enough that I settled down—to my studies, at least. I took up parachuting, hang-gliding, river rafting; you name it, if it sounded dangerous, I did it. Not for the thrill of the sport but to prove that I could do them, that I wasn't a coward. Then I met Melissa. Another rebel against parental restraints. No activity was too outrageous for her to pursue. We fell in love and started living together during our last year in college. Our parents were horrified. The day I was offered a job in Saudi Arabia I rushed back to our apartment and asked her to marry me. She turned me down.'

The memory of his hurt and disbelief echoed in his voice. Elizabeth reached over and took his hand. They walked along in silence, their entwined hands swinging between them. Smoke drifting from the picnic pavilion mingled with the pungent aroma of sweet clover.

'Melissa wasn't in love with me. She was intoxicated with rebellion, the fun of upsetting her parents, the slightly naughty thrill of living with a man. My proposal was a rude awakening for us both. I guess the difference was that I was trying to prove something to myself while Melissa was trying to prove something to her parents. The idea of moving clear across the world to live panicked her. She moved home that same day—and never told me that she was pregnant.'

'Oh, Andrew, no!'

'She knew that I was conventional enough that I would have wanted marriage, and apparently she had this exaggerated belief in my powers of persuasion. Her parents were easily convinced. They didn't want their darling daughter taken from them to the ends of the earth.'

'When did you find out about Linda?'

'A few months ago. I suspect that Melissa's new husband persuaded her to contact me.' He shrugged. 'Maybe she felt that she had nothing to fear from me now that she's married. At any rate, she wrote to my parents and they forwarded the letter to me overseas. Needless to say, I was stunned. A seven-year-old daughter whom I'd never heard about. The first thing I did was call Melissa and tell her that I wanted to see Linda, and the second was to inveigle a job back here in the home office for a while.'

'It must have been as big a shock for Linda.'

'She knew all along. Not the whole story; but Melissa had told her that I lived in the back of beyond and that was why I couldn't communicate with them. She seemed to find it entirely natural. I suppose that one day she'll have to hear the whole story, but I'll leave that to Melissa. I guess I owe her that much for not poisoning Linda's mind against me.'

'I don't think you owe her anything—but,' Elizabeth added reluctantly, 'there's no point in starting a feud which would hurt Linda more than anyone else.' After a moment, she asked, 'How can you talk about her so calmly? I'd be furious.'

'I've already thrown my tantrum. After I received the letter I got stinking drunk and went on a rampage that should have lost me my job and my friends. Fortunately, everyone was understanding. But not too unhappy to see me leave, I'm sure.'

'I feel so terrible,' Elizabeth said in a low voice. 'I should never have been so quick to misjudge you. Can you ever forgive me?'

Andrew lifted their linked hands and brushed her knuckles with his other hand. 'When I left your house this afternoon I swore that I'd never speak to you again. Then I remembered what you'd answered when I'd asked you why you'd helped me that night. Because I'd needed help, you had said, and the look on your face was so astonished, as if it were the stupidest question you'd ever heard. And I realised that, to you, it was. You were worried about Linda and you acted, regardless of the consequences to yourself.' He raised her fist to his mouth and lightly kissed it. 'How can I be angry with a woman who was only thinking of my daughter's welfare?'

It was a question that didn't require an answer, for which Elizabeth was grateful. She stood at the edge of the steep bank and watched a pair of mallards swim to the near shore. Across the river a large black dog debated crossing the river, only to be whistled back by his master. Black birds squawked overhead. Elizabeth took a deep breath and turned to Andrew. 'I was so unhappy when Hannah told me about Linda, and I thought that you had behaved badly.'

'Why?' he asked, looking intently down into her face.

'Everyone keeps saying that I saved your life. I don't know that I did that, but I do seem to have this sort of proprietorial feeling towards you. I'm not sure that I can explain it. When a woman gives birth she wants her child to be the best. In a way, I feel as if I've given birth, or re-birth, to you and, discovering your character was blemished ... I don't know, it somehow made my actions seem less worthwhile. Oh, I know I'm explaining it badly and it sounds silly, but, well, do you see what I mean?'

They were back at Andrew's car. He held the door as she slid into the passenger side. 'Perhaps we've both misjudged each other. I remember accusing you of being irresponsible.'

'And treating everything as a joke,' she reminded him.

Sitting behind the wheel, he gave her a long, scrutinising look. 'Sometimes I think that you are the most responsible person I know.'

'And other times?'

'At other times I know you have the most reprehensible sense of humour of any person of my acquaintance.'

Somehow Elizabeth didn't think that now was the time to suggest to Andrew that perhaps his sense of humour could use some adjustment, too. Instead she meekly agreed that some ice-cream would be pleasant. The hand of peace had been extended, even if not quite wholeheartedly, and far be it from her to slap it away. From lonely rebel to rejected suitor—Andrew had always taken life too seriously. He'd never learned to have fun along the way. He might not be the black monster she'd painted him, but his personality still could use a little improvement. She wouldn't be satisfied until Andrew could laugh at himself as easily as he laughed at her.

Once in Michelle's, Andrew led the way towards the back of the long room. There were a number of customers, one of whom immediately waved them over to his booth. Vince Hunter. Elizabeth didn't recognise the woman with him until Andrew greeted her.

'Bunny. Vince.' Andrew stood aside for Elizabeth.

She slid into the booth beside Vince, aware that the other couple were giving them highly speculative looks.

'Well, what a surprise,' Bunny said. 'I thought you had tickets to the play at the Pikes Peak Centre tonight, Andrew.'

'When you turned me down last week I couldn't face going alone, so I handed the tickets over to my parents.' He smoothly changed the subject. 'What have you two been up to?'

Elizabeth concentrated on her menu. Bunny obviously had both men at her beck and call. Elizabeth didn't think she'd ever seen Vince look quite so besotted. Apparently he'd met his match in Bunny.

Bunny was answering Andrew's question. 'You'll never believe it.' She gave a charming giggle. 'Vince has been introducing me to some of the seamier bars in town.'

Elizabeth arched an eyebrow at Vince.

He shrugged. 'She was curious.'

'Now I'm curious, Bunny. Did you enjoy yourself?' Andrew asked.

Bunny giggled again. 'At first it was deliciously risqué, but it got pretty boring after a while. They kept doing the same old thing. Then one girl started— well, never mind. Anyway, it made me hungry for ice-cream, and so here we are.'

Even her confession was charming, Elizabeth thought. Not to mention a blush that gave her the appearance of a slightly naughty teenager. No wonder Andrew and Vince were looking at her with the fond approval of two adoring uncles. It didn't seem fair— even Elizabeth found herself liking the other woman. Bunny was charming, witty, and, if she was aware of her sexual appeal, she certainly made no effort to exploit it.

'Do you mind?' Elizabeth asked Andrew later as they walked back to his car.

He didn't have to ask what she meant. 'Vince and Bunny? No.'

'I liked her; I didn't think I would.'

'Don't let that brunette bombshell exterior fool you. Bunny is more than the sum of her parts, as provocative as those parts may be.'

A statement calculated to provoke, Elizabeth decided. She refused to give Andrew the satisfaction. She slanted a look from under her eyelashes. 'Vince was watching her with that satisfied air of a magician who's produced a bunny from his hat.'

Andrew laughed. 'Poor Vince. I think he's met his Waterloo. Of course, they'll get married. Do you mind?'

'No, but how can you be so sure?'

'I know Bunny. She has a strict moral code. No sleeping with clients, and no sleeping with a man unless she loves him and intends to marry him.'

'Clients?'

'Sure. Bunny is an accountant. That's how we met. She's been doing my taxes for years; the ins and outs of overseas stuff is her speciality. That sexy exterior hides the mind of a calculator.'

Elizabeth giggled. 'Just what Vince has always insisted never existed. A respectable woman he can display in public and a sexpot he can take to bed in private. Somehow I think they'll make a happy couple. Maybe the third time will be the charm for Bunny.'

'You really mean that, don't you?'

'Why wouldn't I? Oh, you mean because Vince and I dated. I told you, that never meant anything but convenience.'

'Convenient for Vince, maybe, but how could it be convenient for you? He was using you,' Andrew said.

'As I was using him. Vince was a comfortable date. He never demanded more than I was willing to give. A woman who's looking for neither a good time nor a potential mate doesn't exactly have men standing in line to escort her around.'

'Why aren't you looking for a potential mate? After years of taking care of your brothers and sisters, is it that you don't want any part of starting your own family?'

'Of course not. I love children and want my own. They can be horrible little pests but there is such joy and satisfaction in watching them grow and learn and develop into their own personalities.'

'I suppose your parents' unconventional marriage has soured you on the institution.'

'Not at all. I hope to get married some day. And not the kind of marriage that works for my parents.' She gave a little laugh. 'Anna Belle says I'm frightfully old-fashioned. And I guess she's right. I want a full-time partnership—I just don't want it right now. I don't have the time or the energy that a really good marriage needs. And, let's face it, what man would want to move into that zoo where I live?'

'You could move out.'

'I can't. Maybe in eight or ten years, when Julia no longer needs me.'

They pulled up in front of the Asher house. 'Aren't you sacrificing your whole life for your family?'

'I'm only twenty-four. There's plenty of time.'

At the front door, Andrew held it shut when Elizabeth would have gone in. 'I've been thinking about something that you said earlier, about Linda and me being strangers. I was an only child and I'm afraid that I don't have any experience around children. I worry that I'll do something wrong and alienate her for all time.'

'All you have to do is love her, Andrew. The rest will come in time.'

'You know about children. You could help me.' His upraised hand forestalled her comment. 'Linda likes you. I've seen the way the two of you are together. You are also the final authority on everything.

''Elizabeth says'',' he quoted in a high, childish voice. 'You could teach me a lot. We need help.'

She couldn't refuse after that. Because there was no denying the truth of Andrew's last statement. He and his daughter obviously had not the slightest idea of how to go about getting to know each other. 'All right. We could start Saturday, if you're free. How about a trip to the zoo?'

Elizabeth decided that it would be difficult to determine which delighted Linda more—the zoo or the fact that she was on an outing with her father. All three of them laughed at the giraffe display as one after another of the long-necked creatures swayed towards the fence, their long black tongues unrolling in anticipation.

'They want to be fed,' Elizabeth explained. Handing a note to the nearby attendant, she collected a stack of biscuits and handed one to Linda. 'Here. Hold it through the fence.'

'Do they bite?' Linda asked. Reassured that they didn't, she sidled up to the fence.

'I would have bought those,' Andrew said in an undertone to Elizabeth.

She looked at him in surprise. 'They were only a dollar.'

'You're my guest,' he insisted.

'Oh, for goodness' sake, you can buy the next stack.'

'Don't you think that one is enough?'

'Do you?' She nodded towards Linda who was gingerly sticking a biscuit through the fence. As a large giraffe approached her, the small girl lost her courage and jumped back, dropping the biscuit to the ground inside the pen.

Elizabeth handed her another. 'Try again.'

This biscuit followed the fate of the first, as did the next few, but finally Linda clenched her teeth and hung on to the last biscuit until the giraffe took it on his tongue. 'He got it! He got it!' She jumped up and down. 'Can I have more?'

'Linda, we have the whole zoo yet to see,' her father said.

'Surely, one more stack, now that she has the knack of it,' Elizabeth suggested.

'The giraffes aren't the only animals here,' Andrew said. 'The lions and bears are just as interesting and I want Linda to learn as much as she can while she's here.'

'Oh, why didn't you explain that we were here to be educated?' Elizabeth asked, pinning an innocent expression on her face. 'Linda and I thought that we were here to enjoy ourselves.'

Without a word Andrew wheeled around and stomped over to the attendant. Returning, he handed Linda a biscuit. 'Would you like one too, Elizabeth? I want to make sure that you have fun.'

'Why thank you, Andrew. I'd love one.' She joined Linda at the fence. When she thought that Andrew had pouted long enough she turned to him. 'There's one biscuit left. Care to feed it to this big guy?'

'No, thank you.'

She tapped the biscuit against her chin. 'I'll bet your mother would tell me your middle name.'

Andrew snatched the biscuit from her hand and held it through the fence.

Linda clapped her hands in glee when the large giraffe deftly took the food. 'Isn't this fun?' she cried. She took Andrew's hand and pulled him up the hill behind her. 'What's next?'

'Let's walk to the top and start there,' Elizabeth suggested.

As Linda raced ahead, Andrew gave Elizabeth a shamefaced look. 'I guess I need a lot of help with this father stuff.'

'You just have to learn to be a little more flexible,' Elizabeth said.

She was quickly to learn that flexibility didn't come easy to Andrew. When they had entered the zoo he had picked up a brochure, and now had their entire visit mapped out. Unfortunately for his plans, Linda had other ideas. When he wanted to head for the alpine animals, Linda wanted to ride on the old wooden carousel. He consented to her ride grudgingly, but the combined efforts of Elizabeth and Linda could not get him to join them on the old horses.

'Andrew, this carousel was built in 1925. Do you know how few original wooden carousels exist in the United States today? You really should ride on it,' Elizabeth said.

'Carousels are for children.'

Elizabeth made a face and followed Linda inside the enclosure. 'You'll never know what you missed,' she said after their long ride.

Andrew ignored her comment, pointing down the path to their left. 'The bears are next.'

'Oh, the lions!' Linda cried as she darted off the trail in another direction.

'This is not a very efficient way to see the zoo,' Andrew complained as they exited the cat house.

'We're going to miss things if we keep running aimlessly about.'

Linda swung their clasped hands. 'Look. The monkey house. Let's go there next.'

'But we haven't seen the bears or birds of prey yet,' her father objected.

Linda's eyes opened wide. 'Do birds pray?'

'Birds of prey are large birds that eat other birds and small animals.'

Andrew and Elizabeth both laughed at the expression of disgust that covered Linda's face at Andrew's explanation. 'Never mind,' he said. 'Lead me to the monkey house.'

The noise and the smell in the monkey house were overwhelming, but the antics of the animals soon distracted them. The babies quickly had Linda and Elizabeth cooing with delight.

'What are those two doing?' Linda asked as she watched a large male pull a female towards him.

'Playing,' Andrew said hastily with a quick look towards Elizabeth.

She swallowed her amusement and directed Linda's attention to a juvenile who was swinging on a trapeze. In another cage a tiny infant clung to the furry neck of a large female as she climbed up to a high platform. There she sat and, plucking the baby to her lap, commenced grooming him.

'Where's the daddy?' Linda asked.

'I'm not sure. Maybe he's one of those on the other side of the cage,' Andrew said.

'Maybe he is around the world,' the little girl suggested, 'too busy to see his baby.'

Andrew thrust his hands in his pockets. 'Maybe.'

Linda raced ahead. Andrew stood staring into the cage.

From the bleak look on his face, Elizabeth guessed that Linda's comment had upset him. She tucked her arm into his. 'Isn't it wonderful the way that children can enjoy themselves so wholeheartedly? You can just see what a lovely time Linda is having today.'

'And after she goes home and I go back into the field . . . will she be thinking that I'm too busy to mess with her?'

'Of course not. It will be different this time, Andrew. You can keep in touch with her. Write her letters, send her little trinkets, even call her occasionally. There will be more vacations. And don't forget your parents. Their love will be another string that binds her to you. Surely her mother, having gone this far, will support your claim and encourage Linda to love and respect you.'

He gripped the railing in front of him. 'She's never called me Daddy. I haven't had the nerve to ask her to. Or to ask her if she calls Melissa's new husband Daddy.'

'She always calls him Ted when she talks about him,' Elizabeth said quickly. 'Or "Mama's new husband".'

'And me?'

'I've never paid any attention. I mean, if she called you Andrew I would have noticed.'

'She doesn't call me anything,' Andrew said.

'Did you ever think that she might be nervous, too? Maybe she's waiting for you to tell her what to call you. Imagine that you're only seven years old and a stranger is introduced to you as your father. How would you feel?'

'Strange, I guess.'

'Give her time, Andrew. You have the rest of your lives. Besides, is a name so important? Sometimes I call my father "Max" and sometimes I call him "Dad", but I always love him. And that's something you can't force. You can only love her and hope for the best.'

'This parent stuff isn't easy.' He gave her a half-smile. 'It's helped me understand why my parents raised me as they did. Funny how my mother nags at me not to be so protective of Linda.'

'I suppose that the generation gap gives her more perspective,' Elizabeth said.

'I'm hungry.' Linda had returned.

'You've already had popcorn, candy and a drink,' Andrew reminded her.

'I'm hungry again.'

Back outside Andrew looked around. 'I don't see much in the way of a place to eat.'

'There's a stand there with hot dogs,' Linda pointed out.

'Don't you think you've had enough junk food for the day?'

'A hot dog sounds good to me, too,' Elizabeth said. 'I'd offer to buy them myself, but ...'

Andrew glared at her as they sat on a bench in the shade. Linda was out of earshot, feeding the remains of her bun to a begging ground-squirrel. 'You're not only a bad influence, you're infuriating as well.'

'Oh, Andrew, it's just one day. She can go back to drinking carrot juice and eating megadoses of spinach tomorrow.'

'A balanced diet is important, especially for a growing child.' He bit decisively into his hot dog.

'Of course it is. But occasional junk food won't hurt her. Don't turn it into alluring forbidden fruit.' Elizabeth turned her attention to a peacock strolling past, his tail-feathers spread in glorious exhibit. Spotting a peahen, the cock raised his ornate tail-feathers high and began rattling the lower quills in his back. Elizabeth giggled inwardly. For some reason the blustering cock reminded her of Andrew, but she doubted that he'd appreciate the comparison. The peahen ignored the male and walked away.

'Now the hippos,' Linda cried, running up to them.

'She's inexhaustible,' Andrew murmured.

But even Linda eventually wore herself down, the heat and the hills taking their toll. 'My tummy feels funny,' she announced as they threaded their way through the car park.

Andrew gave Elizabeth a look that clearly said, 'I told you so.' 'No wonder, all the junk you ate.'

Elizabeth fastened Linda's seatbelt as she sat between them in the front seat. 'Here. You're just tired. Lean against me and we'll be home in no time. Remember the tiger that roared just as we walked by?' For the rest of the drive she diverted the child's attention with amusing recollections.

Andrew pulled up in front of an unfamiliar townhouse. 'My place,' he said in answer to a look of enquiry. He pressed a button opening the garage door and they drove in. 'I'm not sure I'm up to funny tummies yet,' he explained.

'Coward.' She gave Linda a little squeeze. 'How about if I help you take a quick bath? That will make you feel better and your father can heat you up a little soup.'

The programme was quickly carried out. Elizabeth sat at the dining-room table with Linda while she finished off the last of her bowl of soup. Andrew was making noises in the kitchen.

Linda put down her spoon and yawned.

'I think it's bedtime for you, young lady,' Andrew said from the kitchen doorway with a laugh. 'Tell Elizabeth goodnight.'

'OK.' She slid obediently off the chair and walked into Elizabeth's outstretched arms. 'Goodnight. I'm glad you came with us to the zoo.'

Elizabeth hugged her tightly. 'Me, too. I had a wonderful time.'

Linda turned to Andrew. 'Goodnight,' she said in a polite voice. 'Thank you for taking me to the zoo.'

'You're welcome. Sleep tight.'

Elizabeth stared in disbelief as the little girl disappeared down the hall. She turned to Andrew. 'That's it? You don't kiss her goodnight or tuck her in?'

'I asked her when she first came if she needed me to help her get into bed and she said no, that she was a big girl.'

'Being tucked in isn't the same as being helped. She just didn't want you to think that she was a big baby. If you don't tell her you want a kiss, she probably thinks you don't.'

'May I have a glass of water before I go to sleep?' Linda had returned.

Andrew fetched her a glass. When she finished she handed it back to him. 'Goodnight.'

'Linda.' He hesitated. 'Do you suppose that I could have a hug goodnight?' He held out his arms and she moved shyly towards him.

It wasn't much of a hug, but it was a start. They had seven years to make up for, Elizabeth reminded herself. She gave Linda an encouraging smile as she walked by her. The little girl stopped and gave Elizabeth another hug, then, still in the shelter of her arms, turned and looked at Andrew. 'I had a wonderful time today—Daddy.' The last word was said in a tentative voice.

Andrew froze. Then he grabbed the little girl from Elizabeth's arms and tossed her up in the air. 'So did I. C'mon. I'll tuck you into bed so that this time you'll stay there,' he growled in mock menace.

Elizabeth could hear Linda giggle as the pair went down the hall. Andrew was learning.

She had her bag in her hands when Andrew returned.

'Where are you going?'

'Home. Now that Linda's safely in bed . . . you're lucky she didn't throw up all over you—tossing her in the air when her stomach is already upset.'

'Oh, hell, I forgot all about that.'

Elizabeth laughed at the stricken look on his face. 'Apparently no harm done, but you'd better be careful about those impulses,' she teased.

He took her bag from her hand and dropped it on the sofa. 'Dinner is no impulse. I put steaks out to thaw this morning. The junk food that you two were chowing down today may be OK now and again, but I need real food. Red meat to replace all the blood I lost.'

'I haven't even asked how your shoulder is,' Elizabeth said, smitten with remorse.

'Better, but I still need help tossing a salad.'

'I have a feeling that you're playing on my sympathy.' She put on the apron that he handed her. 'Seriously, how is it?'

'Healing fast. Luckily the bullet went in high and no bones or major blood vessels were hit. Even the muscles didn't fare too badly.' He saw her struggling with the apron strings and moved behind her to tie them. 'I'll never be able to repay you for all you've done.' His hands came to rest on her shoulders. 'Not just for coming to my aid that night.' His hands tightened. 'Did you hear her? She called me "Daddy".'

Elizabeth reached up and covered one of his hands. 'She's a sweet child.'

'What lucky star guided you into my life just when you were needed? Or did the guardian angel of hopeless fathers send you?'

She laughed and turned the conversation into less embarrassing channels.

The day at the zoo must have mellowed him, she decided. Talk flowed easily at the dinner-table as Andrew entertained her with stories of exotic places. 'I've been out to California a couple of times, but I've never been farther east than the Kansas border,' she said. 'I envy you your travels.'

'It's not all seeing the pyramids by moonlight or sampling gastronomic goodies at Harrods in London. I spend a lot of time in areas where it's searing hot or bitter cold. I've had to deal with flies, impure water, disease, poor sanitation, crime . . . if you have an urge to travel, take a guided tour. Even *you* shouldn't be able to get into trouble that way.'

'And always have someone saying "Go here, do that, look at this"... no, thank you. If I ever get the chance to travel, I want to do it on my own so that I can go where and whenever the spirit leads me.'

'It will probably lead you straight into trouble.'

'What an old fuddy-duddy you are,' Elizabeth marvelled.

Andrew leaned back in his chair and studied her over the rim of his glass. 'I will say one thing about some of the locales where I've lived. The women know their place.'

Elizabeth refused to take up his challenge. 'Which reminds me that my place is at home, in bed.' She pushed back her chair. 'It's been a lovely day. Thank you for including me.'

Andrew stood up. 'Tomorrow. Maybe you could join us again.'

'Well, I really——'

'Please. You could bring one of your sisters. Julia, isn't it?' He gave her an ingratiating smile. 'You can't leave us in the lurch now just as I'm getting the hang of it. I still need lots of help.'

It was impossible to refuse when Andrew put it like that. And the next couple of weeks proved the truth of his assessment. Andrew definitely needed help. Sometimes it seemed to Elizabeth that for every step forward he took, he took two backwards. A unique nature programme on television that Elizabeth recommended was missed because Andrew didn't believe in watching television while eating and he refused to be flexible about their dinner schedule. Sleep-overs for Linda were arbitrarily denied on the grounds that she wouldn't get enough sleep. The schedule that Andrew handed to Elizabeth to help her plan Linda's day was flung back in his face, along with the sample menus he presented to her. Even worse was the struggle to avoid being caught in the middle between Linda and Andrew as she tried to point him in the right direction without arguing in front of the child. She might have given up in despair, except for one thing. Every decision Andrew made, no matter how wrong-headed it was, was made solely on the basis of what was best for Linda. They might disagree on what that was, but Elizabeth never doubted that Andrew loved his daughter and was sincere in his efforts to become the best father that he could.

She didn't realise just how far Andrew had travelled down that particular road until the night of the annual family talent show.

CHAPTER FIVE

ANDREW looked around the crowded basement, shock and displeasure warring on his face. 'I thought that this was just for family,' he said in a strangled voice.

Elizabeth arched an inquisitive brow. What was his problem? 'That's how it started out,' she said, 'Chan and I saying a poem for our parents, and they would sing a little ditty or something. It sort of grew into the big production it is now. Friends, neighbours...I'm so glad that your parents could come.'

'Linda asked them,' he said absently, before bursting out, 'Nobody told me there'd be so many people.'

Elizabeth gave him a puzzled frown. 'What difference does it make?'

'Linda talked me into doing an act with her. Something that she saw on television. I'm going to look like a fool.'

'Don't be silly. Even Max participates. Everyone here is an amateur. It's just good fun.'

'What do you do?'

Elizabeth could feel the warm colour steal over her face. 'I don't. Perform, that is.'

'Why not?'

'After many years of suffering through my talentless performances the family voted unanimously to make me stage manager and in charge of refreshments. Max spoke for all when he said that he could handle my monotone version of "I'm a Little Teapot" when I was five years old, but that if he had to listen to me murder George Gershwin or Irving Berlin one more year he was going to murder me instead.'

'My fears exactly,' Andrew said grimly. 'An audience full of critics.'

Elizabeth laughed. 'You don't understand how bad I was. Can't sing, can't dance and all thumbs when it comes to playing an instrument. For a couple of years I tried reciting poetry or reading a play, but I always got the giggles.'

'I can well believe that.'

'Anna Belle pointed out that this is a talent show and that everyone should use the talent God gave them. Since mine seems to be for managing people and cooking...'

'What about your mother?'

'She helps with costumes and designing the sets.'

Andrew looked even more despondent. 'I'm going to be sick.' His eyes lit up. 'That's it. I'll tell Linda that I'm too ill to go on.'

Elizabeth shrugged. 'I'm sure she'll understand. Just because she's probably been counting on the two of you doing something together...I mean, it's not as if you were close, like a real father and daughter, or anything like that.'

'Damn you.' Andrew stalked away.

Elizabeth swallowed her smile. Poor Andrew. It wasn't easy for him when his pride and dignity clashed head-on with his blossoming love for his daughter. Whatever act that Linda had wheedled her father into doing, she only hoped it wouldn't make him look too foolish. She resolved that she wouldn't laugh no matter how strong the temptation.

In spite of the usual hitches, false starts and moments of panic, the evening's programme was successfully entertaining. Max began with a rousing version of Polonius' advice to his son, Laertes, marred only by a pointed glance at Tommy when he reached the part about borrowing. Georgia accompanied Chan and Paige on the piano as they sang a charming duet before she obliged the audience with several classical piano tunes. Tommy had the audience laughing and gasping in wonder with his juggling feats while Abigail, in a dress that Scarlett O'Hara would have killed for, beguiled everyone with her strong rendering of a medley of Broadway show tunes. Laura provided laughter of another sort as she brought on Sam and Barney, who took one look at the huge audience and obstinately refused to perform in spite of numerous dog biscuits. When she gave up, muttering dire threats, Susan and Julia bounced on to the mock stage dressed as kittens, their tumbling antics almost as amusing as the directions they hissed at each other in the mistaken belief that no one else could hear them.

That left only Linda and Andrew. Elizabeth immediately appreciated Linda's idea. Andrew sat on a chair while Linda sat on his lap portraying his wooden puppet. Their stage patter was partly television rehash and partly a seven-year-old's idea of comedy. When their act ended with Andrew receiving a pie in his face, the entire room exploded into laughter. The twosome took their bow. Linda was so obviously pleased with herself, while Andrew was so clearly dying of embarrassment, that the contrast served to send the audience into further gales of hilarity that died down only when Abigail, who was the Mistress of

Ceremonies, announced that there would be a short interval while the scenery was set up for the play.

Elizabeth quickly grabbed Andrew's arm and guided him upstairs to the kitchen, where she handed him a damp towel in place of his ineffective handkerchief.

'Well?' he demanded.

'Well what?'

'Did I make a fool of myself or not?'

Elizabeth tried in vain to control her betraying face muscles.

'Never mind,' he said. 'Go ahead and laugh before you bust a blood vessel trying not to.'

Elizabeth took the towel from him and wiped a smear of whipped cream from above his eyebrow. 'Linda was so proud of you. She'll be talking about it for months.'

Andrew snorted. 'So will half of Colorado Springs.'

Elizabeth dabbed behind his ear. 'I was proud of you, too.'

'Any fool can take a pie in his face.'

'Sure. But you minded so much. Yet you still did it—for Linda.'

'For Linda?' Andrew asked in an odd voice. He grabbed the hand that was wiping his chin. 'Two months ago I wouldn't have even considered participating in something like this, daughter or no daughter.' He brushed his lips across the back of Elizabeth's hand. 'That night you found me, did you put some kind of magic spell on me while I was unconscious?'

'Don't you mean a curse?' she teased. She could feel her pulse racing as Andrew stared down at her, the blue in his eyes darkening to midnight.

'Maybe I do,' he said, before his mouth slowly covered hers.

She couldn't stop the giggle in time.

He frowned down at her. 'What now?'

'You taste of whipped cream.'

Andrew grabbed the towel from her and Elizabeth watched in puzzlement as he smeared whipped cream all over one finger and then tossed the towel into the sink. At the expression on his face, she stepped hastily back. Andrew stopped her with one arm around her waist. Her eyes widened in alarm as he brought his cream-covered finger to her face. 'What are you doing?' she asked.

'This.' He iced her lips. 'You'll taste like whipped cream, too. Now laugh.' The last was spoken against her mouth and then Andrew was licking the cream with his tongue and his lips sucked on hers with little erotic tugs.

Elizabeth didn't feel the slightest urge to laugh. Andrew hadn't kissed her since the day they'd been caught by the sprinklers. She'd told herself that she didn't care, that theirs was a different kind of friendship. Now she found herself hardly knowing what she was doing as she spread her hands against Andrew's chest. Even through his shirt, his body heat warmed her palms. The voices from the basement faded away until the only sounds were their mingled breathing and the drumming of Andrew's heart. She could feel the rapid beat of his pulse—or was that her own blood pounding?

Andrew lifted his head. 'You're not laughing.' He traced her full lower lip with his finger.

Traces of cream clung to his skin. Without pausing to think, Elizabeth stuck out her tongue and licked his finger.

He snatched his hand away. 'You're driving me crazy.' His voice had grown thicker. 'My life used to be so normal.' His lips returned to hers.

'Dull,' she said, when she could breathe again.

'Sensible.' He pressed little kisses at the corners of her lips.

'Rigid.' She burrowed into his shoulder, denying him access to her mouth.

'Respectable.' The word was a whisper in her ear as he nibbled on her ear lobe. One hand gripped her tightly while the other wove through her hair and tipped back her head.

'Stodgy,' she managed, before he recaptured her lips in a determined move that sanctioned no defiance. Not that she had the slightest desire to defy him. Not when his kisses aroused such warm, delicious sensations all over her body. Her bones were melting, her body flowing into the contours of his.

Andrew dropped his arms and stepped back. 'Abigail is calling everyone back to their seats,' he said.

It took a moment before his meaning sunk into Elizabeth's bemused brain. 'Oh. The play.' She turned blindly towards the basement door.

Andrew's hand on her arm halted her. 'Vinegar and baking soda,' he said.

'What?'

'Vinegar and baking soda. Two substances that are innocuous enough on their own, but shake them together and you can create quite a mess.'

'Am I supposed to understand something by that obscure scientific observation?'

'Not all chemical reactions are good. There's no place for a woman in my life.'

Elizabeth gasped in outrage. 'Of all the egotistical things to say... are you insinuating that I want to be in your life? As far as I'm concerned, you're nothing more than a man whom I met quite accidentally, and if it wasn't for the fact that I happen to like your daughter very much and feel that she deserves a father who has at least a modicum of human feeling, I wouldn't care if I never saw you again.'

Andrew raised his eyebrows. 'Your kisses say differently.'

'And just what do they say, Mr Know-it-all?'

'That you enjoy kissing me.'

'So what? Can't a woman enjoy kissing as much as a man does? I suppose your kisses mean that you want to form some kind of permanent attachment with me?' The look of horror on his face would have answered her question even if he hadn't quickly denied it. 'You men. You think you're so wonderful that every woman on earth wants nothing more than to marry you. It so happens that marriage is the last thing on my mind, and, even if it wasn't, let me assure you that you're the last man on earth I'd ever contemplate marrying.'

'Is that so?' Andrew retorted, obviously stung by her words. 'And what's wrong with me as marriage material?'

'I want a man who knows how to laugh.'

'Of course,' he sneered. 'What else should I expect from a woman who doesn't have a serious bone in her body?'

Anna Belle's face peered around the basement door. 'We're waiting for you two. We could have started without you,' she added, 'but you were shouting so loudly that we didn't think we could hear the actresses.'

Wicked pleasure shot through Elizabeth's veins at the dark flush of embarrassment that flooded Andrew's face with her mother's words. Her satisfaction was short-lived, as Anna Belle gave her a critical look. 'Elizabeth, you might want to wash your face before you come down.'

Ignoring Andrew's snort of laughter, Elizabeth marched over to the sink. When she followed Andrew and Anna Belle to the basement she ostentatiously sat across the room from him. The words from the play flowed over her as she replayed the scene upstairs over and over in her mind. Andrew had some nerve, thinking that she was interested in him personally. And just when she was beginning to believe that deep within him was a genuine person with a great sense of humour bursting to escape the rigid persona that he'd developed over the years.

She risked a glance across the room. Andrew appeared to be concentrating on the happenings on the stage. Judging by the grim look on his face, the play was not a comedy. The audience howled with laughter. Surprised, Elizabeth switched her attention to the front of the room.

Susan was obviously a princess. Laura appeared to be her suitor while Julia seemed to be dressed as a witch or wicked stepmother. Linda walked off the stage leading Barney. Just what part Andrew's daughter was playing, Elizabeth couldn't tell. She'd missed too much of the play. The plot had something to do with star-crossed lovers. Susan sat on the lower branch of a fake tree, listening to words of love from below. Suddenly she lunged from the tree and Laura clasped her to her somewhat unmanly bosom and they fell to the stage. At that moment Linda ran out with a sprinkling can and sprayed them as they lay entwined on the ground. The curtain came down to the accompaniment of the audience's laughter and applause. Elizabeth belatedly cursed her inattention. What had those girls said? Her only hope was that on one else realised that at least parts of the play were borrowed from real life. Cautiously she looked across the room at Andrew. He glared back at her.

She should have known he'd blame her. Though how he could . . .

'Didn't you read the damned play before you let them do it?' Andrew hovered furiously behind her as she urged another piece of cake on Mrs Clairmont, the owner of the dachshund.

'Of course not. Coffee, Mr Blake?'

'I thought you were responsible for them.'

'They wanted it to be a surprise.' She handed a plate to the next neighbour in line. 'Yes, Mrs Wilson, the play was awfully clever. I think all the girls had a hand in writing it. No, I can't imagine where they got their ideas.'

'I can,' Andrew hissed in her ear.

'I need to refill the coffee-pot.' She walked into the kitchen. 'You're making too much of it.' There was no need to look to know that Andrew was dogging her footsteps, determined to unleash all his anger on her.

'Too much. Too much! My daughter sees me rolling on the ground with a half-naked female and then tells the whole world and you think that I'm making too much of it. Words fail me.'

'Not noticeably.'

'Sure. Laugh. What's it to you if I'm the laughing stock of Colorado?' he asked bitterly.

'In case you have forgotten,' Elizabeth said, pouring fresh coffee from the huge urn into the smaller silver pot, 'there were two of us rolling around on the ground.'

'To my eternal regret. I suppose it's too much to hope that you intend to do anything about this.'

'Actually, I intend to do several things.'

'What? Publish their play in the newspaper, giving us credit for inspiring them?'

Elizabeth concentrated on wiping up a small puddle of spilled coffee. 'First, I'll take the girls aside and explain to them about rudeness and invading other people's privacy. Secondly, the next time I intend to roll half-naked——' she placed sarcastic emphasis on the last word '—on the ground, I'll make sure that I'm not under someone's window. And thirdly——' she paused in the doorway between the kitchen and dining-room '—I'll give thanks that they didn't see you lathering my lips with whipped cream before you licked it off. Just think what they could have done with that scene.' The door swung closed behind her. But not before she'd had one very satisfactory glimpse of the look of startled chagrin on Andrew's face.

'You don't know how I envy you.'

Elizabeth almost dropped the coffee at the unexpected voice in her ear. 'Mrs Clairmont, I didn't see you.'

'Let me help you, dear. There's always so much going on over here. So much laughter.'

'I hope we're not disturbing you,' Elizabeth said hastily.

'Oh, no. I enjoy listening to all the goings-on. I can pretend that I'm in the middle of it.' She sighed. 'Since Fred died, it's been awfully quiet at my house. I had four boys, you know.'

Elizabeth didn't know. Mrs Clairmont had only moved into the neighbourhood during the past winter. She chided herself for not visiting the woman before. 'Where are they now?'

'All over the place. Only two of them married and no grandchildren. They're waiting, they say. Women and their careers. Oh no, dear, not your mother. She's an artist. Artists are expected to be different. And, besides, she has you to run the family. That's what I miss. Lots to do to keep me busy. I enjoyed cooking and cleaning and making life smooth for Fred and the boys.' She grimaced. 'I just thought I'd get to do it for a few more years. I'm only fifty-three—too young to be put out to pasture.' She glanced over her shoulder. 'So nice, that young man of yours. It's obvious how much he cares for his little girl, don't you think? What a good husband he'll make you.'

Elizabeth involuntarily looked behind her. Andrew gave her a mocking look before engaging in conversation with Max. Elizabeth grimaced inwardly. He'd heard Mrs Clairmont's words and was quick to appreciate that not everyone viewed him as negatively as did Elizabeth. She hastily assured the older woman that there were no marriage plans in the offing.

Unfortunately, Mrs Clairmont was not the only person who jumped to an erroneous conclusion. By the end of the evening Elizabeth was wishing that she'd never met Andrew. Honesty forced her to agree with observations that he was a conscientious and concerned father, but she was heartily sick of trying to convince everyone present that the two of them were not romantically involved. Even Andrew's mother seemed to give her hand a significant squeeze before introducing her to Andrew's father. Her own parents were even worse.

'So, there's nothing between you,' Max said. 'Too bad. I like him.'

Elizabeth bestowed a glance of fond exasperation on her father. 'It takes more than that.'

'Are you happy, Elizabeth?'

'What an odd question; of course I am. Why do you ask?'

'Time passes so quickly when one gets older. When you came to me with the ridiculous notion of taking over the household reins I thought it would merely be for several months. Julia was only a baby. It wasn't until tonight that I realised how much time has gone by. Your mother and I . . . we've been selfish.'

'Don't be silly. If I weren't happy, all I had to do was tell you so.'

Her father studied her face for a long moment. 'I hope that's true, honey. I don't know what we'd ever do without you.'

Elizabeth gave him a big hug. 'You know I'd never be happy if I weren't bossing all of you around.'

Max looked over to where Andrew was conversing with Anna Belle. 'He doesn't look like a man who'd let you have everything your way.'

'Since the question doesn't arise——' Elizabeth began.

Her father laughed and walked away.

Anna Belle was next. 'He's more serious than you are, but I think that you can loosen him up.'

'Not you, too, Mother!'

'I have this fantastic idea for a wedding dress that's been simmering in the back of my mind for ages.'

'Let it simmer,' Elizabeth said. 'Maybe it will come to full boil by the time Abigail is ready to walk down the aisle.'

'He's not at all the type I would have selected for you. Which only proves that even mothers can be wrong.' She patted Elizabeth on the shoulder and drifted away.

Elizabeth rolled her eyes skywards and gave up. There was no point in protesting any more. They would all see for themselves when Andrew made himself scarce in the future. She wouldn't be at all surprised if Linda didn't show up in the morning.

In this she failed to do Andrew justice. Linda was deposited at the Asher front door at the usual time. The first words from her mouth were a prettily worded apology for invading Elizabeth's privacy and for embarrassing her. Close querying disclosed that Andrew had had a long discussion with his daughter. Linda's cheerful demeanour indicated that Andrew had been serious but not intimidating. Elizabeth could scarcely contain her surprise. Just when Andrew had been at his most infuriating and she was ready to give up on

him, he showed flashes of humanity. Not that it
necessarily followed that just because he was rude and
insulting to her he'd be a rotten father; but her experience with Andrew would have led her to believe
that he'd rant and rave and storm at Linda, rather
than merely explain and instruct.

Elizabeth decided to give herself some of the credit:
it was gratifying to realise that she was having some
influence on Andrew. Sometimes she felt as if he was
partly her own creation. She'd found him, saved him
and was in the process of reshaping him into a person
worthy of her efforts. It was with this thought in mind
that she waylaid Andrew when he returned for his
daughter. There was nothing like praise to reinforce
positive behaviour.

'I'm very impressed. You must have handled Linda
beautifully last night. She understood what she'd done
wrong and was properly contrite without being the
least bit sullen or angry.'

'Surprised you, didn't I?'

'I've never doubted that you want to do the best
you can for your daughter.'

Andrew gave her a sharp look before sitting beside
her on the porch swing. 'I don't think that I want to
delve too closely into that statement.'

Elizabeth shoved the swing into motion with her
toe. 'I only meant that what happened here last night
was a mistake, but that's no reason for it to interfere
with my helping you to develop a better relationship
with your daughter.'

'Am I to understand that you are still willing to
spend time with us in spite of the fact that I attacked
you last night?'

Elizabeth could feel the hot colour steal over her face. 'I never accused you of that. I admit reciprocating——'

'Reciprocating. I'll have to remember that word the next time a woman presses so hard against my body that she practically touches my backbone...not to mention kissing——'

'Are you trying to provoke me?'

'Let's just say that I'm learning more from you than how to handle my daughter.'

'If you mean how to kiss,' Elizabeth retorted, 'it seems to me that you already have plenty of experience.'

'Which is more than you seem to have had.'

'Meaning?'

Andrew gave the swing a big push. 'It's obvious to the meanest intelligence. You're ready for an affair.'

'An affair!' That sudden dip in the middle of her stomach had nothing to do with Andrew's words. It was merely the swift motion of the swing.

'Sure. For what—six years?—you've been cloistered here with your family——'

'Hardly cloistered.'

He ignored the interruption. 'At an age where other women are enjoying heady freedom and sexually experimenting and learning what it means to be a woman, you've been stuck here at home and——'

'I have not been stuck. And how do you know whether or not I've been experimenting? For all you know about it, I may have had hundreds of lovers.'

Andrew brushed aside her claim for the nonsense it was. 'If you really do plan to go on with your sterile existence for the next eight years, as you claim, an affair might not be a bad idea.'

'I suppose you plan to offer yourself.' Her tone of voice left no doubt as to her opinion about that.

Andrew clamped his arm around her shoulders, imprisoning her in the swing. 'Why not? Look at the merits of it. I have no intention of getting married, but I'm not unappealing. You have no intention of getting married at this time, but...' he looked down at her, trailing a finger lightly across her cheek to pause at the corner of her mouth '...we don't exactly turn each other off.'

Elizabeth's heart skipped a beat. 'I don't believe that we're even having this conversation. It—it's ridiculous.'

'You're probably right.' He stood up. 'Where's Linda?' He went into the house.

He left Elizabeth in a state of total confusion. Shock, astonishment, irritation, and, she admitted it, a small amount of hurt, all jostled for a place in her emotions. Andrew couldn't be very interested if he was so easily dissuaded. Not that she wanted to have an affair with him. Still, no woman liked to think that she was so—so dismissable.

The next man she saw lying injured on the ground could darn well stay there. Andrew had been nothing but trouble from that moment at the rest-stop when she'd heard him call to her. Catapulting himself into her life and stirring up discontent. Who did he think he was to try and change the way she lived her life? Just as she was trying to change his life, a little voice chided her. That was different: Andrew needed changing. It was for his own good. Even Andrew's mother admitted that he could do with a little humanising. Well, maybe that wasn't exactly correct. She'd said that Andrew was too structured in his approach to living—which was really the same thing.

Look at how he'd behaved at the zoo. And the night
of the talent show. Andrew's problem was that he
risked neither his emotions nor his pride.

The incongruity of that notion struck Elizabeth a week
later, as she glanced at him lying nearby. Andrew
might not be willing to risk his heart with a another
woman, but there was no denying that a female barely
three feet high had completely stolen it away. Watching
his increasingly confident overtures towards his
daughter had gladdened Elizabeth's heart. He was so
determined to be a good father. Not that Linda posed
any difficulties. She was as eager to be loved as
Andrew was to love her.

Elizabeth smiled with contentment. Max's suggestion of a picnic had been a good one and she was
happy that he'd included Andrew and Linda. Her nose
would probably be tinged with pink by the time she
returned home, but that would be a small price to pay
for such a lovely day. Even now the sun shone brightly
through the trees overhanging the small stream, its
rays glinting off spider silk high above the water.

From further up North Cheyenne Canyon came the
faint cries of the others. Tommy had proposed a hike
to Helen Hunt Falls and even Paige had declared that
a short walk would do her good, so the entire family
had set off, Chan watching his pregnant wife protec-
tively. Elizabeth had volunteered to stay behind with
Hewie, while Andrew, declaring that the earlier rock
climbing had totally exhausted him, remained with
her.

'Helen Hunt. Wasn't she an author?'

'Yes. She used to be buried in South Cheyenne Canyon but they moved her grave some years ago. Too much tourist traffic destroyed the peace.'

'It's certainly peaceful here.'

'Yes.' The rushing water muted the sounds of traffic and other picnickers. 'You should have gone with the others. Once over Helen Hunt Falls, the trail runs up and over Silver Cascade Falls. They are beautiful.'

'Too lazy. It's not dangerous, is it?'

'The rocks there are, but the trail is safe and Max will keep everyone on it.'

'Your father isn't what I expected. When you said that he lived across town I assumed that he wasn't a very concerned father, but he actually spends quite a bit of time with his kids.'

'Together and singly,' Elizabeth agreed. 'Family is important to all of us. All the kids bicker among themselves, but let an outsider threaten one of us, and——'

'United we stand.'

'That's right.'

'Do you think that he believes that life will always be this good?' Andrew asked with a nod towards Hewie.

Elizabeth looked down at the small toddler sleeping against the curve of her stomach. 'Babies have their moments of frustration just like the rest of us. Poor Hewie. Little does he knew that he's about to be knocked off his perch as king of the mountain. Once the new baby arrives, he'll suddenly be the older brother.'

'Is that how it was for you? How old were you when Abigail was born?'

'Four. But, of course, I already had Chan. Anyway, I didn't think of Abigail as supplanting me. It was more as if my mother had given me a new doll to play with. I enjoyed all the babies.'

'You ought to have your own.'

'And someday I will.' She spoke softly, bending over Hewie to straighten the clothes that he'd tangled beneath him as he'd rolled over. 'I suppose you're going to start all that again about how deprived I am.'

When Andrew didn't answer, she glanced over at him. His eyes were closed, his chest rising and falling as rhythmically as Hewie's. It was nice to know what a soothing effect she had on men. What would it be like to be a Bunny, with looks and a figure that stopped men dead in their tracks? Or a Sandy with exciting men pursuing her and a glamorous career at her fingertips? She studied Andrew's sleeping form. As usual, one hank of hair had slipped down over his forehead. Even asleep there was strength in his face. Without touching him she knew that his chin would rasp against her skin. With that heavy beard he must have to shave at least twice a day.

The thought occurred to her that Andrew would fit Sandy's definition of an exciting man. Strong, attractive, intelligent, with an interesting career that sent him all over the globe. Nice. Look at how hard he was trying with his daughter.

And sexy. Very sexy. She brushed away a fly that started to land on his nose. No, he didn't look sexy. Sleeping, he looked vulnerable. The sexy was in her own imagination. Because too often at night when she closed her eyes she remembered the feel of Andrew's face between her breasts, the way his beard had scraped her skin. She remembered the way he'd kissed her the night of the ball, the hardness of his body beneath hers on the lawn, the heat from his hand on her breast. His lips licking the whipped cream from hers. Her breasts swelled at the erotic images she'd conjured up, the tips pushing against her knitted suntop.

It was fortunate that Andrew was sleeping. He made a little sound, one perilously close to a snore. If Sandy were sitting here, she'd make sure that Andrew wasn't snoozing beside her.

Sandy! Elizabeth wished she'd never gone to Denver to meet her. Her life had been perfectly satisfactory until then. Not for one minute had she ever felt that she was missing out on anything. Not until Sandy had gone on and on and on about her wonderful life. And the men...

None of the boys or men Elizabeth had dated had received much more than a kiss from her. And when was the last time that any man had tried for any more? Vince had always been content with a chaste kiss on the cheek. Was it possible that Andrew was right? Could she have been subconsciously suppressing sexual longings that she didn't even know she had? Look at how quickly she'd responded to him. Wouldn't it be ironic if she ignored these longings now and then, later, when it was convenient for her to get married, discovered that she'd repressed her sexual side for so long that it no longer existed? Elizabeth was aware that a great deal of the success of her parents' unusual marriage arrangement was due to the fact that they shared a healthy animal appetite for sex.

Sex! Was that all she could think about? It certainly had never been a topic that had overly occupied her in the past. It was all Andrew's fault for bringing such discord into her life. She should have gone to bed with one of her boyfriends years ago. Why couldn't she have lost her virginity in the back seat of a car like some of her friends? Maybe then she'd know what all the shouting was about and she wouldn't feel so discontented now. Darn it. Marriage just wasn't on the books for her at this time, but Andrew's suggestion of an affair was ludicrous.

Two large black and orange butterflies darted by, one almost on top of the other. Elizabeth wondered if they were mating. Insects, birds, animals; they all mated by instinct. There was no waiting around to fit coupling into some convenient schedule.

CHAPTER SIX

'I saw Bunny the other day when I went in to sign some tax papers. She was sporting a rock so big that the sparkle practically blinded me.'

'I thought you were asleep.' Elizabeth glanced down at her front. Fortunately her body was behaving again.

'Merely resting my eyeballs. What had you so deep in thought? Judging by the expressions on your face, nothing pleasant.'

'Was the diamond from Vince?'

'Yes. Do you mind?' Andrew asked.

'How many times do I have to tell you that I don't?'

'Did you ever sleep together?'

'Not that it's any of your business, but no.'

'Why?' His eyes were closed again.

'Friendship between a man and a woman does not have to have sexual overtones.'

'He's an idiot if he never made a pass at you.'

'Is that a way of excusing your own behaviour?'

'I didn't realise that it needed excusing. I don't remember getting my face slapped.'

'I knew you'd get back to that,' Elizabeth said. 'I am not wasting away for want of an affair. I've managed this long without hopping into bed with some man, and I'm sure that I can continue to do so quite successfully.'

Andrew rolled over and opened his eyes. One dark eyebrow rose a fraction of an inch. 'Never?'

'Don't tell me that that's a sin in your book.'

'No. I'm surprised to hear it, that's all.'

'I don't know why,' Elizabeth said. 'You're the one who pointed out that my inexperience was justification for us having an affair.'

'I don't think I put it quite like that. However, it is interesting how frequently you manage to bring the subject up. Have you been considering it?'

'Of course not. I know you were merely trying to annoy me.'

The sound of voices came around the bend. The rest of the family was returning. Andrew stood up and brushed off his trousers. 'I thought that I was offering my services.'

'I wouldn't want you to sacrifice yourself on my account.'

'It would be no sacrifice.' He turned towards where Linda was waving to him. 'Believe me. No sacrifice at all.'

She couldn't sleep. The house was quiet: Anna Belle busy in her studio, Chan and Paige retired for the night, the older kids out, the younger asleep. Nothing on television appealed to her—everyone on all the programmes seemed to be paired off. 'Everyone is, except you and me, Coconut.' She softly brushed the white cat's fur as she slumbered on Elizabeth's lap. Even Coconut had had at least one family, according to the veterinarian they'd taken her to when they'd adopted her. 'So, you had one lover, anyway. Is that why you're so content to lie quietly at home every night now?' Did cats dream of their past amorous lives? She knew that Sam dreamed of chasing rabbits. His legs would churn and he'd bark in his sleep. He wasn't allowed to roam now. Running loose was what had got him run over by a car in the first place. Elizabeth had found him beside the road. Luckily for the owners, they'd never answered Elizabeth's advertisement for them. She'd been furious, but now Sam was a much-loved, if slightly rowdy, member of the family—an assessment she knew that Andrew would agree with.

Andrew. Darn her habit of picking up injured strays. It only got her in trouble. Sam and Barney were the least of the culprits. Andrew was the one whose violent arrival into her life had caused such turmoil. Her intentions had been innocent enough. His survival had come first, of course. Then it had been a matter of claiming him as her creation, feeling that helping him had given her proprietorial rights; that it was almost her duty to interfere in his life and shake him up, make him more human. What an egotistical fool she'd been. Pandora opening her box had nothing on Elizabeth Asher. People who interfered in nature usually got exactly what they deserved. Trouble.

And there was no denying that Andrew was trouble. The serpent in the Garden of Eden. She looked down. Coconut was heavy on her lap. Admit it: she was twenty-four years old and lonely. With all her family and all her friends, her life lacked something. Odd, she'd never noticed it before. It was all Andrew's fault. Andrew and his talk of her needs. Andrew and his offer of an affair. Andrew and his kisses. Anger and discontent rose in her breast. Deep within her, other warmer, needier sensations grew and she shifted uncomfortably on the sofa. 'Damn him.' Coconut lifted her head at Elizabeth's words, jumped indignantly from her lap and stalked across the room. 'Not you,' Elizabeth apologised. 'You never cause any trouble.'

Remembering those words, Elizabeth could only appreciate their irony as she apprehensively awaited Andrew's arrival the next evening. He was going to be irate and Coconut had been the innocent cause of all the trouble.

She met Andrew at the front door. 'I won't blame you for being furious, and I know that it's all my fault even if I did tell her not to go up, that I'd get Coconut down, but then the phone rang and I never should have gone to answer it because by the time I'd gone back outside it was too late and...and...' Elizabeth gulped. The look on Andrew's face was not encouraging. 'I was sure it was broken but the doctor said that it's only a sprain and there's no concussion or anything, but she's lying down now and——'

'You're babbling. Tell me what happened or find someone who can.'

'Linda fell out of a tree. She's up in Julia's room,' she called as Andrew swept past her and took the stairs two at a time. By the time she caught up with him he was sitting on the edge of the bed smiling at his daughter.

'What's this I hear about you trying to fly without wings?'

Linda gave him a tentative smile. 'I thought you'd be mad at me.'

'Why should I be mad at you?'

'Because Elizabeth told me not to go up that tree and I disobeyed. She told me that the branch wouldn't hold me and she'd get a ladder, but Coconut was crying.'

Andrew smoothed the hair back from her forehead. 'Coconut?'

'Elizabeth's white cat. Julia said that Elizabeth saw some boys throwing her from the top of an apartment house to see if she'd land on her feet. Elizabeth was so mad that she yelled at the boys and took Coconut away from them and brought her home, and now she's Elizabeth's cat. Julia told me how scared Coconut gets up high now, and when that mean old dog chased her up the tree she cried and cried. I know Elizabeth told me to wait, but Coconut was crying so hard.' The small girl swallowed hard. 'She's such a little cat,' she said in a tiny voice.

'How's your arm?' Andrew asked her.

'Hurts.'

'Then I think you've probably learned your lesson, don't you?'

Linda nodded, then looked down at the sheets clutched in her fists. 'Are you going to yell at Elizabeth? Laura said that you'd be really mad at her 'cos she's 'sponsible for me.'

Andrew looked over his shoulder at Elizabeth standing in the doorway. 'I think she feels bad enough about what happened, too.' He stood up. 'C'mon. I know you'll want to phone and tell Grandma about your latest adventure.'

Elizabeth trailed after them as they went down the stairs. She couldn't believe that Andrew would be willing to leave the matter there. At last his restraint drove her to action. Urging Linda on to the car with Julia's help, Elizabeth blocked Andrew's departure. 'Thank you.'

'For what? Refusing to bite off your head?'

She felt the embarrassing colour sting her cheeks. 'That and being so understanding with Linda. Will—will you let her return tomorrow?'

'If she's in pain, I'll stay home from work. Otherwise, she'll be back.'

Quick tears sprang to Elizabeth's eyes. 'Thank you.'

Andrew leaned down and pressed a soft kiss against her lips, before murmuring outrageously, 'How could I ever persuade you to share my bed if I didn't have an excuse for bothering you every day?'

'Andrew! If you think . . .'

He was already getting into his car. Leaning across Linda, he called through the open passenger window, 'One question.'

'What?' Elizabeth asked warily.

'What happened to the damned cat?'

'She came down from the tree while we were at the hospital,' Elizabeth admitted, 'none the worse for her scare.'

Andrew grinned. 'Let that be a lesson to both of you. Never interfere with nature.' He paused. 'Or fight it.'

The phone call wasn't totally unexpected.

'I thought you'd want to know that the patient is resting comfortably,' Andrew said.

'I'm really sorry.'

'Don't worry about it. She learned her lesson at not too heavy a cost. Besides, both her grandmother and grandfather rushed here straight away right to fuss over her, somehow convinced that she was some type of heroine. In vain did I point out that the cat managed to rescue herself.'

'Well, I'm happy that she wasn't seriously injured.'

'Me, too.' His voice changed. 'That isn't really why I called. Have you thought any more about what I said?'

'No,' she lied.

His low laugh came clearly across the line. 'No? How do you know what I'm talking about?'

'I assume that you mean that less than subtle comment about fighting nature,' she said.

'Then you *were* thinking about it. How about discussing it over dinner tomorrow night? If Linda is feeling OK.'

'There's nothing to discuss.'

'I'll pick you up when I come for Linda. She's been invited to spend the night with her grandparents.'

'I don't see——'

'Save your arguments. You might need them.'

The dial tone buzzed in her ears.

'You look beautiful,' Linda said in an admiring voice.

'Elizabeth is the most beautiful person in the world,' Julia boasted.

'My mama is beautiful too,' Linda answered.

Elizabeth smiled at the two girls watching her get dressed. 'She must be. She has such a lovely daughter.'

'I called her last night,' Linda said in a voice filled with self-importance. 'All the way across the country. Daddy said I could.'

'Was she upset?' Elizabeth pretended that it was a casual question.

'No. She said that she fell out of a tree when she was five and broke her wrist.'

'I broke a finger when I was three,' Julia offered.

'You did?' Linda was impressed.

Elizabeth turned the conversation back into more interesting channels. 'What else did your mother say?'

'She misses me. And I should be good. And she was happy that I like Daddy.' Linda gave Elizabeth a shy look. 'I was scared before I came. Mama said he was nice, but ...'

'But you didn't know him,' Elizabeth said.

Linda nodded. 'You like him, too, don't you?'

'She's going to eat dinner with him, isn't she?' Julia asked.

'I told Mama about you,' Linda said.

Elizabeth put down her eye-liner. 'What did she say?'

'She said that not many little girls were lucky enough to have two daddies and two mamas.'

'Stupid—Elizabeth isn't your mama,' Julia said.

'That's what I told Mama. She just laughed. What do you think she meant, Elizabeth?'

'Is that a car door? Why don't you two run down and see if Linda's daddy is here?' Coward, she said to herself as they ran out through the door. Why didn't she just explain to Linda that her mother had only been teasing her? Didn't Andrew's former fiancée re- alise that her betrayal had soured Andrew forever on the idea of marriage?

She heard his voice downstairs. Now that he was here she was having second thoughts. Second? More like twenty-fifth thoughts! Going to dinner with him was a mistake. The dress was a mistake. A backless halter-top, it was bound to give Andrew ideas. She'd selected it on impulse because the white fabric em- phasised her light, golden tan. Her hair was another mistake. She should have braided it on top of her head. Hanging loose, curled around her face—it was

too sensuous. And why in the world had she dabbed
on so much perfume? He'd be positive that she had
seduction on her mind. When the truth was . . . no,
she didn't care to think about what the truth was. Not
tonight. Not when her pulse was racing, sending erotic
wafts of fragrance past her nose. Not when a million
butterflies were darting around in her stomach. Not
when her bones had turned to jelly. Elizabeth sat down
on the bed and strapped a pair of white sandals on
her bare feet. Grabbing a sweater, she took a deep
breath and headed downstairs.

Andrew drove efficiently, with the economy of
movement that she'd come to recognise as character-
istic of him. He'd been home and changed before
picking her and Linda up, and Linda was deposited
at her grandparents' home with a minimum of fuss
and time. Andrew apparently arranged his life so that
nothing was left to chance. Which made her question
the wisdom of agreeing to dine with him this evening.
Not that she'd actually agreed. Which pointed up one
of the basic differences between them. Andrew etched
his plans in concrete. Elizabeth traced hers in dust.
Easily disturbed by the breezes of chance—normally.
Not tonight. Tonight she intended to be friendly, yet
keep Andrew at a distance. Then he would realise that
there was nothing more between them than a chance
encounter and mutual concern for the welfare of his
daughter.

She stole a glance at him as he sat behind the wheel.
Why had she ever thought that pink was an effemi-
nate colour? The silky-knit fabric delineated muscles
that rippled each time he shifted the car's gears or
turned the wheel. His shirt sleeves were rolled up, ex-
posing black hairs on his forearms. The sight sent her

gaze to his face. He'd recently shaved. The breeze
through his open window sent a trace of aftershave
wafting her way, a masculine scent that suited his
rugged appearance. In spite of spending the past few
weeks indoors he sported a healthy tan, courtesy of
his recent job in the Middle East. Deep squint lines
radiated out from his blue eyes, the mark of a man
who spent a good deal of time outdoors. He would
be dangerously attractive if she weren't quite aware
that neither one of them was the least bit interested
in pursuing a relationship that was so obviously wrong
for them both.

The car slid smoothly into Andrew's garage.

Elizabeth looked at him in surprise. 'I thought we
were going out.'

Andrew opened her door. 'Easier to talk here. If
it's not loud music, it's the waiter always bothering
you in restaurants. Do you mind?'

'Would it make a difference?' she asked as they entered the house.

'It would mean a lot of food down the drain.' He
lifted the sweater from her shoulders and laid it across
the back of the nearest chair.

The warmth of his hands clung to her as she followed him into the kitchen. Containers of food lined
the refrigerator shelves. 'Don't tell me you spent the
day cooking?'

'Hardly.' He handed her a glass of white wine. 'All
it took was a few minutes on the phone and one stop
on the way home. Salmon pâté, a few select cheeses,
a couple of breads, wild rice salad, marinated cherry
tomatoes, cold roasted Cornish game-hens and a fresh
strawberry cheese tart.' He spread some pâté on a thin,

crusty slice of bread and popped a piece into Elizabeth's mouth. 'A feast fit for an angel.'

She swallowed. 'A whole choir, if you ask me. Ummm . . . delicious.' She had accepted a second bite before his comment hit her. 'Why an angel?'

'I don't know. It seemed appropriate. Maybe because you look like an angel in that white dress.' He took her glass and set it on the counter. 'Let's get this over, with so that we can enjoy dinner.' Backing her up against the cabinet, he took her hands and brought them up to meet at the back of his neck.

His intentions were obvious. Elizabeth closed her eyes to blot out the deep gleam in his. His lips were smooth and cool and tasted of wine. He slid his hands the length of her arms, across her shoulders and down to her waist. His thumbs barely nudged the tips of her breasts in passing, but that was enough to excite them into straining against the cotton fabric of her dress. Her lips parted at the urging of his tongue and she clung to him as he leisurely explored the softness of her mouth. She knew when his fingers unfastened the buttons down the front of her dress, but her mind was incapable of reasoning why he should be denied. His hand was warm and her breast swelled to fill the cup of his palm. Slowly he moved his hand back and forth, his skin rasping against the tender peak until it was taut with desire. Then, when she thought that she had reached the summit of erotic pleasures, he showed her how wrong she was by lowering his head and sucking on the sensitive tip of her breast. A staggering flame leapt to the centre of her being, there to burn and smoulder with painful intensity. Moaning, she pressed his head tighter against her breast. Andrew's lips released her and trailed hot kisses on her skin up to her neck. Tipping back her head, he recaptured her mouth, while his hands stroked her breasts with a soothing touch. And then a single finger edged between their lips, parting them.

Elizabeth opened her eyes. Andrew's gaze was intense, as if he was memorising the features of her face. Were her eyes as sleepy-looking as his? Her lips felt swollen and she could feel the warm flush that coloured her skin.

A slow smile spread across his face. 'See—that wasn't so bad.'

She buttoned the front of her dress with trembling fingers. 'Would you care to explain?'

'I knew you'd spend the whole evening worrying about "was I going to or wasn't I?", so I thought that I would and then you'd know. A couple of sips of wine, a peek at dinner to distract you, and . . .' He toasted her with his wine glass.

'You mean you planned the whole thing?' She clutched at the glass he handed her.

'I don't believe in leaving things to chance.'

'You're unbelievable. Maybe I wasn't nervous. Maybe I didn't want you to kiss me.'

'I had contingency plans.'

'You're serious, aren't you? You probably had the whole seduction planned down to the smallest detail. I suppose your contingency plans even included allowing for a dress that didn't button down the front.'

'As a matter of fact . . .'

'You should have told me. I could have planned ahead of time, too. Maybe I would have preferred to have had three bites of pâté before we kissed.' She whipped up her anger at the thought of his coldly calculated moves. 'Or maybe I would have preferred you kiss my right breast instead of my left, or maybe——'

'I hope you're not telling me that you didn't plan something of the same nature. That dress and perfume would make a liar of you.'

'Of all the arrogant conclusions to draw, simply because I—I made myself presentable.'

Andrew took her wine glass and substituted a bowl of tomatoes. 'You're annoyed because I didn't pretend to be spontaneously aroused by your beautiful presence.'

She followed him into the dining-room. 'It's not very romantic or flattering to know that being kissed is reduced to the same level as . . . as changing a flat tyre. Step one, step two, step three . . .' She stopped in surprise.

The french windows to the veranda were open, allowing a fresh pine scent to perfume the air through the screened doorway. The dining-table had been shifted to one side of the room and a creamy flokati rug lay on the carpet near the open doors. A small tablecloth in gay florals was centred on the flokati, flanked by two piles of large cushions.

Andrew set the dishes he was carrying on the cloth. 'I thought that we'd have a picnic. Without flies.' His hands captured hers as she handed him her bowl. 'It's not that I'm not overwhelmed by how terrific you look this evening. I am. And I'm gratified by the trouble you went to.' A finger on her lips halted her denial. 'You're beautiful no matter how you're dressed. In a wet, dirty T-shirt or with whipped cream all over your face. Spontaneity might be considered an admirable quality by some, but, quite frankly, making love on

the lawn with the sprinklers going has its limitations
as far as I'm concerned.'

'I didn't come to make love. I came for dinner.'

Andrew brought in the rest of the food and dropped
to the floor across from her. Refilling her wine glass,
he handed it to her. 'Eat. And then we'll talk about
it.'

'No, we won't. I don't——'

He popped a tomato into her mouth. 'After dinner.'

She swallowed. 'Do you always get your own way?'

'No, but I try.' He placed a small hen on a plate
and handed it to her.

'You know what I can't figure out about you? How
does your job fit into this compulsion you have to
plan your life and control events?'

'I'm not sure the two fit together so much as they
offset each other. Gambling and instinct play a large
part in the oil business. I'm in the production end,
and at any given time a hundred variables can crop
up. No matter how many studies the geologists under-
take, there's always a chance of a dry hole. And not
only do I have to take into account the vagaries of
the ground below me, I have to deal with the personalities of the men who work for me. Add weather,
politics, the world market—and the only certainty
about the oil industry is that it's always stimulating.
And that's all the excitement and stimulation I need.
In my off-duty hours, I want life to run smoothly and
efficiently. Planning is the answer.'

'Linda must have thrown quite a monkey-wrench
into your plans.' Sitting cross-legged on the flokati,
she added some rice to her plate.

'These past few months have been a series of
monkey-wrenches. First, the news about Linda. Then

the mugging. Not that I minded unexpectedly gaining a daughter.'

'Especially such a charming one.'

'Yes, Melissa's done a good job. I'm going to miss Linda when she goes back.'

'Have you considered suing for custody?'

'That would be pretty selfish of me.'

'But if her mother doesn't want her around . . .'

'Where'd you get that crazy idea?'

Elizabeth frowned in confusion. 'I thought her new husband—that was why she finally told you . . .'

Andrew quickly understood. 'Not to shove Linda out of the way. Melissa adores Linda. As does Melissa's husband. Melissa only consented to this long stay with me because she felt she owed me. Besides, a single parent in my business . . .' He frowned. 'I'll work out something. Melissa will doubtless have more children, but Linda is all I'll have.'

'You don't know that. You could marry, have other children.'

Andrew shook his head. 'I told you. Marriage isn't for me. Dragging a wife all over the world, away from her family, expecting her to put up with long absences or spartan living conditions. When I was young I thought that such an existence would be romantic, that love would be enough.' He sipped his wine. 'I'm not so naïve now. I suppose that in time I might have deceived myself into thinking that a woman might be happy sharing my lifestyle, but Linda saved me from that potential disaster. No, I'm happy with the status quo. A good job. A lovely daughter.'

'And female companionship?'

Andrew shrugged. 'Not every woman expects commitment.'

'I think that's sad. And unfair to women. Just because Melissa let you down, you think all women are weak.'

'I don't think a woman is weak because she wants some of the basic necessities of life. And who are you to attack Melissa for not wanting to leave her family?'

'That's different,' Elizabeth said. 'She went home because she was afraid to leave. I'm staying because my family needs me.'

Andrew moved the dishes to one side and refilled their wine glasses. He lay back on his cushions, his eyes shut. 'And meanwhile?'

'Meanwhile, I'll go on as I've been. Busy, happy——'

'Discontented. The Country Mouse. That's what you called yourself. You said that your friend Sandy was the City Mouse.'

Elizabeth widened her eyes in surprise. 'I thought you didn't remember.'

'Snippets of your conversation keep popping into my mind.'

She sighed. 'I talked too much that night.' What would he think once he'd achieved total recall?

Andrew reached over and trailed his fingers lightly up and down her bare arm. 'Kismet.'

Her skin tingled where he'd touched it. 'Kismet?'

'Fate, destiny. You came along when I needed you. No one will argue about that. And maybe I came along when you needed me. You just didn't realise it.'

Elizabeth snatched back her hand. 'Are we back to that?'

He opened his eyes, before punching up some cushions behind her back and pushing her into a half-reclining position on them. Leaning on one elbow, he contemplated her over his wine glass. 'Of course we're back to that. What did you think this dinner was all about? I told you from the very beginning that roses were hardly adequate to repay you.'

'Tommy suggested an oil well.' She was beginning to recognise that gleam in eyes half hidden by drooping lids. Her racing heart sent blood pounding in her ears. She had no intention of acquiescing in Andrew's plans, but, since he obviously had no intention of taking her home until he'd outlined them to her, she might as well listen and get it over with.

'He's still young enough to think that money's the answer to everything. Which, in your case, it's definitely not.'

'Go on. What is? I'm breathlessly awaiting your venerable words of wisdom.'

'Humouring me?'

'Isn't that what you're supposed to do with crazy people?'

Andrew bent his head. 'Is that what you're doing when you kiss me? Humouring me?' he asked against her lips.

'Yes.' It was harmless enough. And pleasurable. Her lips clinging to his. His chest barely touching hers. One of his legs flung across hers, the fabric coarse against her bare skin.

'Liar.' He lifted his head, while one hand softly traced the contours of her face. 'You were right about one thing. Sometimes I need female companionship. Like now. I need a woman who has no interest in future commitment.'

'That's nothing to me.' Her heart was threatening to burst through her skin.

'It could be. You're a generous, loving woman. Subconsciously you must have feared those very qualities in any relationship with a man. There's always been the potential that you'd fall in love and want to get married, abandoning your family. So you've played it safe, dating men like Vince Hunter who were no threat to your plans. I don't know why you allowed me to slip past your guard. Probably because of the emotionally-charged circumstances of our first encounter. Whatever the reason, there's a chemistry between us that's explosive. My first thought was to deny it, to stay away from you. Then I realised that I didn't have to, that you were no more interested in a shared future than I am. But that's no reason why we can't grab the moment.'

'Andrew, I'm not——'

'Hush. Let me finish. I'm not criticising your virtue, nor am I treating it in a cavalier manner. We would be very discreet. No one need ever know.'

'It sounds so... so tawdry.'

CHAPTER SEVEN

'I RATHER thought that it sounded practical.' Andrew shrugged. 'But, if you're opposed, then I won't upset you by discussing it any further.' He pushed himself to his feet and grabbed several of the empty dishes.

Elizabeth trailed him to the kitchen, her thoughts weighted down by an inexplicable misery. 'I'm sorry.'

He dropped a quick kiss on her lips. 'Nothing to be sorry about. Look at it as a business proposition that didn't work out.'

'Will you still bring Linda over?'

'One has nothing to do with the other.'

They were back on the flokati rug. She gave him a quick glance. 'I wouldn't have thought you'd give up so easily.'

His eyes were shut again. 'Who said I did?'

'You did! You said you wouldn't discuss it any more.'

'Not discussing the matter and giving up are two totally different things.' He opened one eye. 'Contingency plans are bread and butter to an engineer.'

For some curious reason, Elizabeth's spirits lightened. She had no intention of taking him up on his offer, but discussing it wouldn't hurt. 'I suppose that you had this entire affair planned out.'

'Down to the tiniest detail. Care to hear?'

'Why not? I love a good fairy-tale as well as the next person.'

'Privacy and the need for secrecy were my first concerns. I convinced my mother that I'd be willing to share Linda two or three times a week. Mother's thrilled. She's missed having Linda around, but she hated seeing her lonely. Once she saw how much Linda enjoyed the hustle and bustle of your family, she felt that she had to send her to you. I don't know how you managed to convince my mother in one short visit that you were not only warm and generous but capable of caring for her only grandchild. Mother refused to consider anyone else.' He gave Elizabeth a quick smile. 'Anyway, next was the question of where to conduct our assignations. Colorado Springs isn't that large, and since you've lived here all your life there was always the danger of running into someone who knew you. Everyone's speculation the other night at the talent show pointed out the need for stealth. Finally, I decided that you could come here.'

'Everyone would notice your picking me up all the time.'

'But I wouldn't be. You'd pretend to be meeting with friends and leave home alone.'

'And no one would notice my car here all the time.' There was more than a hint of sarcasm in her voice.

'You wouldn't drive here. You'd go to one of the malls and park, go through the mall, and I'd be waiting on the other side. Here we'd drive right into the garage and come inside without ever showing your face to the neighbours.'

Elizabeth had to laugh at his satisfied air. 'All that planning. Such a shame it's for nought.'

'Persistence is another quality of engineers. I really abhor abandoning a good plan.'

'You have my sympathy,' she said.

'Your sympathy's not what I want.'

Elizabeth braced herself, but the expected onslaught of heavy persuasion failed to materialise. Andrew was the perfect host and entertaining companion for the remainder of the evening. Not once did he renew his suggestion that they have an affair, unless one counted the way he kissed her before driving her home. A kiss that left no doubt in Elizabeth's mind that, however mute Andrew had been on the subject, his mind remained unchanged. So did hers, but that didn't stop her from tossing and turning all night, unable to close her eyes without seeing the hungry gleam in Andrew's eyes as he bent his head.

Lack of sleep made her irritable the next morning and longing to take her irritation out on Andrew. How dared he make such a proposal to her? Andrew, however, stopped his car in front of the house just long enough for Linda to slip out. Elizabeth lay in wait for him throughout the long day, but once again she was thwarted as he remained in his car when he picked Linda up, honking the horn to summon his daughter at a time when Elizabeth was in the midst of dinner preparations and unable to leave the kitchen.

After a couple of days of similar occurrences, Elizabeth realised that Andrew was deliberately avoiding her. Casual interrogation of Linda provided little information: Andrew was busy at work. Elizabeth finally concluded that he had had second thoughts and was too embarrassed to face her. Therefore it came as something of a surprise when Linda announced that Andrew would be picking Elizabeth and Julia up on Saturday morning, to join them for a trip to the fossil beds at Florissant.

Linda's next announcement was more of a bomb-shell. She was spending the night at her grand-parents'. Probably because that lady was coming over again, she added ingenuously.

'What lady?' Elizabeth demanded.

Linda shrugged her thin shoulders. 'Some lady Daddy works with. She ate dinner with him at our house last night. I ate with Grandma. Daddy said they'd be talking business and I'd be bored.'

Business. Elizabeth couldn't help but wonder if the business had been conducted on the flokati in front of open dining-room doors. Andrew had certainly lost no time in finding more willing feminine companion-ship, while remaining true to his claim that Elizabeth's help with Linda had no connection to her refusal to share his bed. Just why she should be irritated at Andrew for reconciling himself to her wishes wasn't a subject that she cared to explore.

Saturday morning dawned hot and dry with sudden gusts of wind shaking the tree limbs and creating fast-moving shadows on the lawn. The air was noisy with the whistling sound of humming-birds shooting from feeder to flower-bed, looking like iridescent bullets as they aggressively defended their territories.

Elizabeth sat on the swing in the screened porch, Julia squirming with excitement beside her. Elizabeth felt like squirming herself. She hadn't talked to Andrew since Tuesday night. Would he bring up the subject of an affair or was his so-called co-worker taking sufficient care of his needs? Not that anything more than curiosity prompted the question. How Andrew spent his evening hours meant nothing to her.

Andrew eyed her pale pink sun-dress with approval as she slid on to the front seat. 'You look as luscious as cotton-candy.' He leaned over and pressed his lips warmly against hers. 'Taste good, too.' Before she could protest at the intimacy in front of the girls, he called over his shoulder, 'Don't you two agree that Elizabeth looks good enough to eat?'

'Like strawberry ice-cream,' Linda said.

'More like pink grapefruit juice,' Julia said. She hated pink grapefruit juice, a fact which she quickly passed on to the others.

Andrew gave Elizabeth a quizzical look. 'Dissension among the ranks?'

'Julia and I had a slight disagreement this morning over dress,' she admitted.

'She's so bossy,' Julia grumbled. 'She was worse than a wicked witch all week.'

Elizabeth could have strangled her youngest sister, but, if Andrew read any significance into Julia's statement, he kept it to himself. The usual summer influx of tourists crowded the highway up Ute Pass and he needed to concentrate all his attention on his driving. Elizabeth was content to ride in silence, occasionally listening to the girlish conversation from the back seat. A small river rushed downstream on their left, brown with sediment from yesterday afternoon's summer squall. The road twisted and turned between high, reddish hills. Elizabeth pointed out to Linda the old abandoned railway with its many tunnels piercing the red rock. Once past Woodland Park the landscape opened up into rolling hills, dotted with orange Indian paintbrush, pink wild geraniums and clumps of yellow daisy-like flowers. On their left, Pikes Peak was still decorated with white crevices of snow, while occasional swales swarming with wild blue iris reminded passers-by of the recent spring melt.

The Florissant Fossil Beds being a national monument, it wasn't surprising that the parking area was already half occupied when they pulled in. The girls hopped up and down impatiently as Andrew paid their entrance fees and picked up a pamphlet to guide them. Julia, as well as Elizabeth, had been several times before and she was anxious to show off her knowledge. With an admonition not to bother others, Elizabeth allowed the girls to bound ahead.

'The path is well marked. They'll be OK,' she assured Andrew, as they stood looking over the vast basin that had been a prehistoric sea.

The girls' laughter floated back to them and Andrew grinned as he watched them climbing down the steep stairs to race past three enormous, excavated fossilised trunks. 'What I wouldn't give for such energy.'

'We don't have to go down. There's a path around the top,' Elizabeth said, showing him. 'These are Sequoias—the largest found in the world. They're thirty-five million years old. Inside the visitors' centre we can see examples of the fossilised plant and insect life they've found around here. Many look no different from what we can see living today.'

'What's that pretty blue flower?' he asked as they moved along the trail.

'Flax.'

'Reminds me of your eyes. Not only the colour but its skittish behaviour.'

'It takes only a minimum of breeze to disturb it because the stems are so slender.' She pretended she didn't hear his personal reference.

Andrew took her hand, entwining their fingers. 'And what disturbs you?'

'I'm not disturbed.'

'Then how come you haven't been able to look me in the eye since I picked you up?'

'You're imagining things. Here's a good look at the shale that covers the area. Millions of years ago volcanoes in this region left plants and animals buried in layers of ash. Gradually the ash hardened into shale while the life-forms within fossilised.'

'Fossil. What's left behind when life has gone. I'd hate to see that happen to you.'

Elizabeth took a deep breath. 'This flower here is a scarlet gilia.'

'That intense pink matches your cheeks when you're upset.'

'Why did we come here if you're not interested?'

'But I am. I'm very interested. Did you think I wasn't?' He took the pamphlet from her lifeless fingers. 'Here we have a fine example of a blue spruce. Look at how blue the new growth is at the end of the branches.'

Elizabeth followed him along the trail barely listening to his instructive monologue. There was no doubt in her mind that Andrew had chosen to misunderstand her question and was letting her know that his proposition still stood. Unfortunately, if she voiced her displeasure, he was capable of insisting that he'd been referring to the Fossil Beds. She wondered about the other woman. 'It's lucky for Linda that you had time to spend with her today.'

Andrew broke off in the reading of a description of juniper to give Elizabeth a look of surprise. 'Why wouldn't I? That's the whole point of her visit, for us to spend as much time together as we can.'

Driven by demons beyond her control, Elizabeth said, 'That would certainly be news to Linda.'

The hand holding hers gripped painfully tight. 'Are you telling me that Linda is unhappy about something?'

'No! She hasn't said anything.' Why had she started this conversation? She should have known that trying to subtly ferret information from Andrew was hopeless. Andrew always wanted all his 't's crossed and his 'i's dotted.

His grip loosened. 'Are you unhappy?'

'Of course not. Sniff this ponderosa pine-tree. It's supposed to smell like vanilla, but I admit I've never been able to smell it.'

'Another on your long list of things you've never done,' Andrew said as he obediently sniffed.

Just then the girls raced up to rejoin them, sparing Elizabeth the need to answer. They were hungry.

Andrew looked at his watch. 'We have a few minutes to browse inside and then we'll go eat.'

'There are restaurants in Cripple Creek nearby, or——'

'I've made reservations at a place in Florissant,' Andrew interrupted.

'I should have guessed. Planning ahead.'

Andrew dropped the pamphlet in the box at the end of the trail. 'Of course. It's the key to my success. I can't abide failure.'

Elizabeth was relieved that lunch in the renovated streetcar offered no opportunity for private conversation between the adults. The girls were full of their morning discoveries and she welcomed their eager— and safe—questions. Andrew sat back in his chair surveying them all as if he were their benevolent patriarch.

After lunch found them back on the road, this time to Cripple Creek and Victor, small gold-mining towns that were once the centre of one of the wealthiest areas in the world. Their first stop was the district museum. Passing the famous mining exhibitions with barely a glance, the girls were entranced by the Victorian room-sets.

Andrew was more interested in reading about one of the notorious town madams. 'You could have made your fortune twenty times over.'

'I don't think I was cut out to be a gold-miner,' Elizabeth said, deliberately misunderstanding him.

He laughed. 'A beautiful woman like you wouldn't have had to soil her hands. There were plenty of millionaires in those days who would have gladly shared their gold. Why, you could have been another Baby Doe Tabor.'

'And look what happened to her. Froze to death, broke and alone, at their worthless mine.'

'Elizabeth, hurry up. The sign says that we can't go up the stairs without you.' Julia's shrill voice was easily heard over the low conversation of the other visitors.

Andrew followed Elizabeth, Linda and Julia up the curved, wooden, cantilevered staircase. On the third floor the girls exclaimed with pleasure over the elegant old dresses, and fell in love with a yellowed, lace-trimmed wedding dress.

'The bride must have been awfully skinny,' Linda said.

'They used corsets to lace in their waists to make them look smaller. Just think, this dress was worn in 1909,' Elizabeth said.

'Didn't her tummy hurt?' Julia was more interested in the practical aspects.

'The best part of her wedding day must have been when her husband took it off her,' Andrew said.

Elizabeth hoped that the girls assumed he meant so that the bride could breathe again. She contented herself with one reproving glance that was countered by one of complete innocence.

Next on Andrew's agenda was a ride on the narrow-gauge railway between Cripple Creek and Anaconda, a route that was lined with old mines silhouetted against the horizon, stark reminders of the past. Elizabeth's head swam as she tried to compute the monetary value of the gold removed from the mines at the present price of gold. 'I can't do it,' she finally admitted to Andrew. 'It's too much. But even then, fortunes were made practically overnight. Of course, some weren't as lucky as others, gambling away their gold and their mines.'

'I think our luck's run out, too,' Andrew said with a nod towards the darkening sky. Since the train carriage was windowless, although roofed, Elizabeth was relieved when the rain held off until just as the train was moving back into the station. Hard drops spattered to earth as the foursome descended and ran laughing for the shelter of the car.

There was little conversation on the ride back to Colorado Springs. The girls were weary and dozed intermittently. Andrew seemed to have nothing to say beyond a few choice comments on the driving habits of tourists. Back in the Springs he pulled into his own garage.

'Why aren't you taking us home?' Elizabeth asked in surprise.

'I promised Linda a full day. We're cooking hot dogs on the grill. Linda's idea, since you obviously love them. My mother said that she'd bring over some potato salad and fixings, and leave them in the refrigerator.'

'Are they joining us?'

'They had other plans.'

Linda was eager to show Julia her room and the girls quickly disappeared.

'You can use my room to freshen up,' Andrew said.

His room was immaculate, the articles on his dresser arranged with military precision. There wasn't even a water-spot on the mirror in the small adjoining room. The only jarring note was her bedraggled image in the mirror. Elizabeth quickly set to work to repair such damage as she could. She was applying a coat of lipstick when she spotted blue lace caught in the wardrobe doors behind her. Moving across the room, she opened the doors. And gasped.

A sheer lace robe trimmed in satin hung over a satin night-gown inset with lace. Its creator might have stolen the blue colour from the flax flowers they'd seen earlier. Impulsively Elizabeth stroked the satin fabric. It was cool and silky and she imagined the gown sliding down her bare skin. The image was as pleasurable as it was sensuous. But only for an instant. Then it was replaced by another image. An unwelcome image. That of some other woman in this gown. Andrew's co-worker. Were her eyes blue, too?

'Glamorous, isn't it?'

Elizabeth whirled round. Andrew stood in the bedroom door. 'I—I . . . it was hanging out . . . the lace . . . afraid it would get ripped.'

Andrew walked into the room, removed the outfit from his wardrobe and held it in front of her. 'A perfect match,' he said in satisfaction. He hung it back.

She couldn't stop herself from asking. 'For what?'

'Your eyes. What else?'

Elizabeth dropped to sit on his bed before her unsteady legs betrayed her. 'It's—it's not for me?'

'Of course it is.' He gave her a tranquil look. 'I know how impetuous you can be. I wanted to be prepared.'

Thank goodness for her knees, or her jaw would have dropped to the floor. 'Are you telling me that you bought that for me just in case I consented to have an affair with you?' At his nod, she closed her eyes in disbelief and shook her head. 'You're incredible. Of all the arrogant——'

'I prefer to think of myself as far-sighted.'

'You act as if it were a question of when, not if.'

The grin on his face was a masterpiece of self-confidence. 'Planning and persistence.'

'Pig-headedness. I said no and I mean no.'

'Then there's nothing more to discuss, is there?' He closed the wardrobe doors.

'I think you'd better take us home.'

'Before we eat? How do you intend to explain that?'

She couldn't. And he knew it. 'How do you intend to explain that outfit to Linda?' she challenged.

'A gift for her grandmother? She's much too young to question any explanation I choose to give her.'

Elizabeth followed him to the kitchen. 'You may as well return it while you can still get your money back.'

'I'm not worried. The question is, if your mind is so made up, why are *you* worried?' He handed her a bowl of potato salad and called the girls to eat. The table was set in its accustomed place in the middle of the dining-room. The flokati rug was not in sight.

The next week was one of the longest that Elizabeth had ever lived through. Although she resolutely asked no questions of Linda, she couldn't ignore the small girl's artless conversation. The information that Linda had spent the night at her grandmother's house again sent a shaft of pain through Elizabeth. If that other woman was wearing her gown . . . She caught herself in disgust. The gown had no more to do with her than did Andrew's amorous activities. Still, there was no denying a small, very small, urge to see herself in that gown.

Andrew, meanwhile, was obviously conducting a hit-and-run campaign. One day he'd drop Linda off with a wave of his hand to Elizabeth; the next he'd come to the door and make provocative remarks about how appetising she looked in the morning. The afternoons were worse. Elizabeth never knew whether to expect a honked summons for Linda, or Andrew to materialise at the kitchen door demanding a tall, cool drink. Drinks that cooled him off even as he heated up her emotions with baited comments and smouldering looks.

'How about a movie on Friday night?' He gave her an enquiring look over his glass.

'I don't think——'

'Doubting your own resolve?'

'Certainly not.'

'Good. I'll pick you up at seven. We can eat first.'

*   *   *

Andrew pulled his car into his garage.

'I should have known that I couldn't trust you,' Elizabeth said.

'I promised you dinner and a movie and you'll get both.'

'I didn't know you meant here.'

'When I pay good money, I want to hear the whole movie. Current audiences are too rowdy for me, so I rented a video tape. Besides,' he stood aside to allow her to enter, 'it's hard to seduce a woman in those minuscule excuses for movie theatres that are presently so popular.'

'I ought to turn around and go right home.'

'But you won't. Because then you'd be admitting that I might be right about you.'

Elizabeth dropped her bag on the sofa. 'Don't think that you can challenge me into your bed. It won't work. Nor will softening my resolution with wine.'

Andrew handed her a goblet. 'I like my women willing and sober.'

'Like your friend from work?' Before he could answer, she rushed on, 'Did she wear the blue nightgown?'

The puzzled look on Andrew's face was quickly supplanted by amusement. 'No, and no. That was strictly business. Did you recruit my daughter as your spy?'

'Don't be ridiculous. Little girls babble all the time. I could hardly tell her to shut up.'

Even Elizabeth had to admit that her disappointment at seeing the dining-room table elegantly set for two was totally incongruous in the face of her stated feelings. Even more ludicrous was her conviction that Andrew was somehow tormenting her when he failed to kiss her before they sat down to eat. Conversation was genial and impersonal. Elizabeth learned more than she'd ever wanted to know about the oil industry. Not that Andrew's stories weren't fascinating. It was merely that, with him having titillated her in public with provocative remarks, when they were alone she'd expected to be besieged by blandishments and seductive charm. Primed for war, she was knocked off balance when Andrew refused to sound the battle cry.

Elizabeth mentally gritted her teeth and set out to prove that she could win the game even if she had to play by his rules. Exhibiting a nonchalance that was at total variance with her inner turmoil, she related one humorous tale after another of life in her family, not even caring that some of the more lurid ones sent Andrew's eyebrows shooting towards the ceiling. She was conscious of his setting traps for her but she managed to evade them all. Her first mistake came as they were eating the delicately flavoured flan that Andrew had purchased for dessert. 'I suppose that we're going to see *Casablanca* tonight.'

The slow, smug smile that crawled across his face instantly apprised her of her error. 'Wouldn't that be a little obvious? One of the most romantic movies of all time. Besides, the hero doesn't get the girl. That certainly isn't in accord with my plans.'

She refused to be baited. 'What are we going to see?'

'*The African Queen.*'

It sounded innocuous enough. Humphrey Bogart and Katharine Hepburn in a war film. But how could she have forgotten Hepburn's role? Rosie, a missionary's staid, virginal sister. A woman who'd subordinated her life to her brother's vocation. And Bogart. A boozy adventurer and river-boat pilot. Thrown together by the whims of war and caught up in the accompanying dangers, they'd bedded together about halfway through the film. Without benefit of clergy. Of course, one could argue that if clergy had been available . . .

Andrew switched off the screen with the remote control. 'Great movie.'

Beside him on the sofa, Elizabeth dabbed at her eyes. 'Do you think they got married when they made it back to civilisation?'

'They were married. By the ship's captain.'

'Would that have been legal? What about licences and things like that?'

'Who knows what the laws were back then. I doubt if they were as rigid as today, when a man needs a licence to kiss a woman.'

'I'd never heard that.'

'Good. Then it must not be true.' Grabbing her around the waist he pulled her over to sit on his lap. 'You and Rosie are a lot alike.'

Elizabeth stiffened. 'I'm not sacrificing my life for my family.'

Andrew tucked her head into his shoulder. 'I was thinking more about full speed ahead and to hell with the consequences.'

'I'm not sure if you're praising me or damning me.'

'When it's a question of rescuing me, I'm definitely praising you.'

'And when it's not?'

'Then, too. Linda has told me in exhaustive detail how your family came to acquire so many pets. You

must be considered the guardian angel of the helpless,'
Andrew said.

'Not exactly that, but I do get angry when I see
people abusing animals.'

'Haven't you ever worried that your dashing in
might have disastrous results? When I think about you
taking Barney away from that man who was hitting
him with a stick, I shudder. What was to prevent him
from using that stick on you?'

'Guilt, and the collective rage of everyone else on
the street. I made sure he knew that I got plenty of
names from people who witnessed the entire episode,
and then I quickly took Barney by the Animal Shelter
for one of their officers to see; plus, my vet docu-
mented his condition when I took him there. And finally, Max went with me to the man's house and we
paid him for Barney and insisted that we get a bill of
sale.'

Andrew grabbed her chin and tipped her face up
for his inspection. 'Impulsive, but not brainless.'

Elizabeth fluttered her eyelids. 'Oh, golly, Mr
Harcourt, you're embarrassing me beyond belief with
all them flattering words.'

'And you, Miss Asher, are tempting me beyond
belief.' He promptly demonstrated just how low his
resistance was.

Elizabeth immediately recognised that this was what
she'd been waiting for all evening. Andrew's lips
against her. His tongue exploring her mouth. His arms
holding her tightly against him. Her heart quickened
with anticipation and she shifted slightly to a more
comfortable position. And in so doing inadvertently
allowed him easier access to her breasts. Or had she
wanted his hand there, warm and possessive? Buttons

were quickly disposed of. That had been another careless error. A blouse that buttoned down the front. Andrew tugged it from the waistband of her skirt and slid his hands up her back beneath the loosened blouse. One quick movement and the lacy scrap beneath was free.

'Thank goodness women don't wear corsets any more,' Andrew said. He slipped the blouse from her shoulders. Lace quickly followed. His eyes glinted with suppressed emotion as he inspected her bare breasts. 'Beautiful.' He cleared his throat. 'Perfect.'

The words were as tangible as a touch and Elizabeth could feel the swelling desire that hardened her nipples. Andrew pulled her against his chest and she delighted in the feel of his clothing against her bare skin. For a while. Then it was not enough. Leaning back she unbuttoned his shirt and slipped her arms inside to glide over the smooth surface of his back. His skin was warm to the touch while his erratic pulse sent waves of masculine scent into the air. His breathing was quick and shallow. As was hers. She slid the shirt down his shoulders, following its path with her hands. Crinkly black hairs teased her palms. His chest hairs captured her gaze, and she wove her fingers through the thick mat until she discovered tiny nubs that turned hard at her touch. With a groan Andrew pulled her back against him and kissed her deeply. She thought she'd explode with feeling as his wiry chest hairs brushed against the sensitive tips of her breasts. And then his fingers were there. First to soothe, but soon to drive her to even higher plateaus of exquisite, tortuous desire.

Disappointment was painfully sharp when Andrew lifted his head. Elizabeth burrowed into his chest, unwilling to let him read on her face the emotions that betrayed her. Not that he didn't know. Only a fool could misinterpret the fact that Elizabeth desired Andrew every bit as much as he desired her.

Andrew tossed her undergarment to one side and covered her bare back with her shirt. Then his arms crossed behind her back and they sat in silence, their mingled heavy breathing and the combined pounding of their hearts the only sounds. 'Now is when I need you to turn the hose on me,' Andrew finally said.

Elizabeth responded with a weak giggle. 'And Barney.'

'Damned dog.' There was no rancour in his voice.

CHAPTER EIGHT

'WHY did you call a halt?' Elizabeth asked. 'If you hadn't we'd probably be in your bedroom by now. I was in no mood to say no.'

'Exactly.'

She was confused. 'But I thought that you wanted...'

'I do. But not that way. Not an impulse brought on by the wine or the moment. You have to decide that going to bed with me is absolutely something that you want. I don't want any regrets or recriminations after the fact.'

'Aren't you worried you may have lost your opportunity?'

'Better a lost opportunity than a lost friend.'

She leaned her head back to study his face. 'You're serious, aren't you?'

He nodded. 'I owe you far more than I could ever repay. Possibly my life. Certainly for taking my daughter and me under your wing. You've enriched both our lives this summer with your caring, your concern, your generosity.' He dropped a light kiss on the tip of her nose. 'And with your love of life. I've never met a person who so wholeheartedly embraces life the way you do.' A finger traced the outline of her jaw. 'When I'm back in the field, hot, tired, depressed, I'll close my eyes and hear you laughing and I'll know that life isn't that difficult.'

Sudden tears formed in the corners of her eyes and she ducked her head to hide them. Why did Andrew's words make her so sad? She should be leaping with joy and satisfaction. Mission successfully completed. Wasn't it? In the relationship with his daughter Andrew had travelled the long road from undemonstrative stranger to loving father. Maybe he still found it difficult to laugh at himself, but he no longer took himself so seriously and he'd learned the value of laughter.

Andrew stretched, in the process moving Elizabeth to one side. 'Time for all good little girls to be home in bed.' He stood up and reached out his hand to her. 'Linda and I are leaving early in the morning. We're going to camp out down at the Great Sand Dunes. We'll be home Sunday evening. If you decide—in my favour, shall we say?—give me a call then.'

'And if I don't?'

'I'll bring Linda by as usual, Monday morning.'

Two days to make up her mind. Two days. It wasn't enough. It was too much. Elizabeth had never before felt this biological need to couple. How could anything she wanted so badly be wrong for her? If only there were someone she could ask for advice.

'Aren't you going somewhere with Linda and Andrew today?' Anna Belle asked in surprise, sitting down at the lunch-table on Saturday.

Elizabeth explained about the camping trip.

'Too bad he didn't take you along. The dunes are so romantic with the moon shining on them.'

'Experience speaking?' Elizabeth asked.

Anna Belle smiled complacently. 'Abigail and Susan were both conceived there on family camping trips.

No woman is resistible in such a romantic setting.' She closed her eyes and gave a dramatic sigh. 'The golden moon, the scent of wild flowers blowing on night breezes, the primitive sound of owls hooting and coyotes howling.'

'The ants, the hike to the bathrooms, the blowing sand salting your food,' Tommy added.

Elizabeth laughed with the others, happy to have the subject changed even as she pondered Anna Belle's words. Her mother almost made it sound as if she thought that Elizabeth's sleeping with Andrew was the most natural thing in the world, with Andrew's reluctance being the only obstacle.

Her father appeared to have reached the same conclusion. 'I hear that you let your boyfriend get away from you this weekend,' Max said on Sunday morning over a family brunch.

'He's not my boyfriend,' Elizabeth said, handing Laura the syrup.

'Then he's a fool.' Max stopped cutting his waffles and pointed his knife at Elizabeth. 'Or are you the fool?'

Elizabeth could feel the hot flush sting her cheeks as the entire family stopped eating to stare at her. 'I don't know what you mean.'

Max glared at Anna Belle. 'You explain.'

Anna Belle made a face at her husband. 'This is the first time in her life that Elizabeth hasn't acted impulsively. Doesn't that tell you anything? Tommy, stop feeding Sam bacon from the table.'

'Mama, you gave Barney a muffin,' Julia crowed. 'And Chan gave Mai Tai a piece of sausage.'

Julia's words turned the conversation into a free-for-all of flying accusations and indignant denials.

Elizabeth ignored the spirited debate. Her family had read more into her friendship with Andrew than she'd realised. To them it appeared to be a foregone conclusion that she and Andrew would walk off into the sunset together. She wondered at their reaction if she suddenly announced that Andrew wanted her to have an affair with him.

She lay back on her bed after brunch and stared at the ceiling. The house was quiet. The family was gone; to a film, to work, to friends' homes. She'd stayed at home to think. But why should that be necessary when her mind was already made up? She crossed her hands behind her head. Lace curtains swayed in the breeze that brought in the scent of freshly-mown grass. Laura was cutting Mrs Clairmont's lawn and Elizabeth could hear the distant whirring of the mower, punctuated by the strident whistling of passing humming-birds. Two of Mrs Clairmont's sons weren't married. Did they sleep with anyone? Or were they still considering it?

Considering it. As she was. And where had that thought come from? Since when had she been considering it? Wasn't she the one who'd insisted from the very beginning that she absolutely was not going to have an affair? The times with Andrew. The dinners at his house. She was only fooling herself if she didn't admit that lurking somewhere deep in her subconscious had been the expectation, maybe even the hope, that Andrew would take the decision from her and seduce her into an affair. He'd certainly exploded that idea. No impulsive decision, he'd insisted. She sat up and crossed to her desk. Andrew would doubtlessly weigh all the pros and cons before he reached a de-

cision. Fine. So would she. Pulling a sheet of paper
from a drawer, she picked up a pen.

Two hours later she tossed the pen down. It was
hopeless. The 'pro' side of the paper was covered with
handwriting. His warm relationship with his
parents...his understanding of his former girlfriend's actions...the fact that her family liked
him...the way that he'd committed himself totally
to having a loving relationship with his daughter. She
smiled as she remembered the pie he'd stoically taken
in his face. The rest of the items were nonsense. Black
hair that always hung over his forehead. Blue eyes
that darkened when he kissed her. The single word,
'kisses'. That hadn't needed any elaboration. Nor did
the fact that he left her breathless, limp and trembling
with desire.

On the minus side was only one comment. Too
structured. There were other thoughts, but she refused to commit them to paper. The dangers of
sleeping with Andrew. What if she became addicted
to his loving? What happened once he left? Because
he would leave. He'd told her that from the beginning. And, finally, the enormity of what she was
contemplating. It went against all her upbringing and
beliefs. Would she want the same for her younger
sisters? A cheap affair carried on in sleazy motel
rooms. Not literally. Andrew would be the perfect
gentleman, thoughtful and discreet. No one need ever
know. It would be their secret. Hardly the romantic
relationship she'd envisaged as a child. She'd always
assumed that one day the right man would come along
and they would live happily ever after. Andrew was
merely a passing ship in the night.

She wished she'd passed him in the night. That fateful night they'd met. Kismet, Andrew had said. Maybe he was right. She had saved him and he was hers. If he left now there would be an incompleteness in the circle that fate had drawn for them. Fate. She snorted. If fate decreed what was going to happen, then she certainly wished that fate would give her some sign so that she could get on with life and stop agonising. Crumpling up the useless piece of paper, she tossed it into the dustbin. She'd known all along what her decision would be.

Andrew was waiting for her call but there was no hint of triumph in his voice. He sounded almost impersonal as he arranged to meet her on Tuesday evening at the shopping mall.

Dressing took extra care. What would appeal to Andrew without alerting her family? In the end she chose skin-tight jeans over pink cotton bikini underwear. A matching pink cotton-knit camisole clung intimately to her skin beneath a loosely knotted floral blouse. She slid her feet into moccasins. The single fat braid down the back of her neck was a concession to her family. They thought that she was going bowling.

She was late. Would Andrew wait? There was no doubt in her mind that he would be a stickler for punctuality.

He was tapping the steering wheel impatiently when she slid breathlessly into the passenger seat. 'OK?' he asked, after one quick look.

'Yes.'

Silence stretched ominously between them as they left the parking lot. Elizabeth squeezed her hands tightly together, willing her heart to slow down. Andrew must hear it in the hushed car. He cleared his throat three times before she realised that he was as nervous as she was. The thought was somehow calming.

'I'd hoped you'd wear your hair down.' His voice was unnaturally loud.

Elizabeth removed the rubber band and combed her hair out with her fingers. 'Better?'

He looked over. 'Much.'

'What now?'

He didn't misunderstand. 'There's champagne cooling in the refrigerator. You can slip into the blue gown while I turn on some appropriate music. Maybe you'd like to dance or talk a little first.'

'Yes, thank you.' She gave a little giggle. 'I'm as nervous as a girl on her first date,' she confessed.

'I plan to take things very slowly,' Andrew said.

The car slid silently into the garage. Elizabeth followed Andrew into the house. He dropped his car keys on the chest by the front door and turned to her. 'Waiting... I thought you'd changed your mind.' He moved nearer and threaded his fingers through her hair.

She toyed with the buttons of his shirt. 'No. I couldn't decide what to wear.'

His hands slid down to cup her bottom. 'I like your final decision. When I saw those hips swinging towards the car...am I going to need pliers to remove your jeans?'

His eyes had changed to that mysterious dark blue that revealed his desire. 'Why don't you find out?' she challenged.

With a low groan he locked her against his body, his lips taking deep possession of her mouth. Elizabeth flung her arms around his neck and answered his kiss with mounting passion. He lifted her into his arms and took her into his bedroom, his mouth cleaving to hers. Standing her beside the bed, he knelt to tug off her jeans and remove her moccasins while she took off her shirt and dropped it to the floor. No words were needed to know that he approved of her underwear. Not that it graced her body long. He was clumsy in his haste but she made no protest. The same vulnerability that had driven her to comfort him in her arms when he'd been in pain compelled her to accommodate him now and ease his need . . .

Afterwards he collapsed at her side, one arm flung over her stomach. His head rested on her shoulder and his breath was rapid puffs of air against her cooling skin. Hemingway was wrong—the earth didn't move. She brushed the lock of hair back from Andrew's forehead. Maybe it was enough for women to know that they gave pleasure to their men. Andrew's breathing was almost back to normal. It was a pity that they didn't smoke. In films that always seemed to take care of this awkward moment. She tried for the light touch. 'I was looking forward to the champagne.'

'Then you shouldn't have sabotaged my plans.'

'Who rushed whom into the bedroom?' She hoped that Andrew didn't hear the faint tinge of pique that had somehow crept into her voice.

He rolled off the bed and walked over to the wardrobe. 'How about a glass of champagne now?' His back was to her as he shrugged into a robe.

'All right.'

The wardrobe door remained open when he left. The blue négligé and gown shouted at her from across the room. Stepping over her abandoned clothing on the floor, Elizabeth was drawn to the wardrobe. The gown's fabric was smooth and silken to her touch. There was no sign of Andrew, and his shower tempted her through the open adjoining door. She welcomed the stinging water against her skin but it failed to wash away the need that ached deep within her.

Andrew had been in his bedroom while she was showering. The blue robe and gown were spread on the bed. Elizabeth dropped her towel to the floor and picked up the gown. It was cool as it slid down her body, caressing her skin much as she'd expected Andrew to. Discontent wove its insidious way into her thoughts and she ruthlessly thrust it aside. Andrew had made her no promises. The lace robe was lovely, but stiff and scratchy. As Elizabeth returned it to the wardrobe, a full-length mirror caught her attention.

Andrew was right. The blue fabric was an exact match for her eyes. The gown might have been made exclusively for her measurements. Thin straps held up smooth satin that moulded her breasts and glided past her stomach and hips before falling loosely to the floor. A large diamond-shaped insert of lace flirted dangerously close to the tips of her breasts, while the bottom point stopped a provocative distance below her belly-button. She twisted to see the back. The gown outlined every curve, every valley.

'Your champagne awaits, Beautiful Lady.' Andrew was lounging against the door jamb, a goblet in each hand. He'd put on a pair of jeans but his chest and feet were bare.

In other circumstances she would have been embarrassed at being caught in front of the mirror, but Andrew's blatant masculinity knocked every emotion but one from Elizabeth's thoughts. Desire flooded through her body. She grabbed the glass he offered and took a big gulp to cool her heated body.

In the living-room slow, dreamy love songs flowed from the stereo. Andrew took the glass from her hand and set it on a low table. She walked into his arms. When the music ended he replaced it with more of the same. Again. And again. The outside world was forgotten. There was only Andrew. The warmth of his back against the palms of her hands. His heart beating steadily against her as he pressed his body tightly to hers. His unique scent. The sensuous feel of his hands slowly gliding over her hips. The cool fabric that separated them was less a barrier than an aphrodisiac. The music clicked off.

'More champagne?'

She shook her head. A few sips had been enough. Andrew was more stimulating than any wine.

He swung her up into his arms. 'Now it's your turn.'

Elizabeth opened her eyes. The room was dark. She must have dozed off. Not too surprising, considering. She stretched lazily on the bed. Muscles that she'd never known she had protested loudly. Her turn, Andrew had promised. A promise he'd faithfully kept. Elizabeth had never dreamed that a man could give a woman such pleasure. Embarrassment flooded her veins as memories washed over her. Abandoned behaviour. A need so intense that she'd begged Andrew for release. Had all those moans and cries really come from her? What must Andrew have thought? She turned to face him. The bed was empty beside her. The dent in his pillow hollowly mocked her and the satisfied feeling evaporated into the air, leaving her empty and lonely. Andrew wouldn't have abandoned her, unless... She closed her eyes in pain. Revelling in her own pleasures, had she failed to notice that Andrew was less content?

She switched on the lamp beside the bed. All her clothing had been picked up from the floor, folded, and placed atop Andrew's chest of drawers. Even the sensuous blue gown had been reduced to a tidy pile of fabric. Andrew's clothes lay neatly beside hers. He must have worked in the dark. He'd missed his shirt and it hung forlornly on a bedpost at the foot of the bed. Elizabeth shrugged into it and padded out of the room on bare feet.

Andrew was in front of the open dining-room doors, his back to her. He was wearing his jeans. Hesitantly Elizabeth joined him. A quick glance from him acknowledged her presence but he didn't speak.

'What time is it?' she asked.

He didn't bother to look at his watch. 'After midnight.'

'Time for Cinderella to leave the ball.' She was proud of the way her voice didn't falter.

'Why did you come in the first place?' His voice was angry, his words an accusation.

Elizabeth took an involuntary step backwards. 'I'm sorry, I...' How did one apologise for inexperience? She could hardly promise to try harder next time.

Andrew threw his champagne glass across the room. It hit the wall with explosive force and Elizabeth realised that he'd been drinking. The bottle on the table was empty.

'Damn it! Don't you dare apologise to me!'

'All right.' She was shaken by the fury in his voice as he grabbed her upper arms with fingers that drilled into her bones. 'But I would like to know what this is all about.'

He flung her away from him. 'Why didn't you leave me be the night you found me? Any woman with a bit of sense would have. But not you. Oh, no. Guardian angel of the helpless, I once called you.' His hand clamped once more on her shoulder. 'I didn't know how close to the truth my words were, did I? Angel.'

'You remembered.'

'Why didn't you tell me before?'

'Tell you what? That you were hurt and needed comforting? That you were delirious from banging your head?'

'What I thought you did—pick me up, bandage my wounds, haul me off to the hospital—that's almost impersonal. But you went beyond mere rescue. You held me—a stranger—to your bare breasts and comforted me. For those few moments, even in my delirium, I sensed that you cared about me as a human being. I couldn't see your face but I felt that you were good and pure and beautiful. Enticing you into an affair made a mockery of those feelings.'

Elizabeth felt as if she were struggling to keep afloat in a sea of bewilderment. She'd anticipated that they might be embarrassed if he ever recovered his memory but she'd never expected anger. 'I'd have done the same thing for anyone.'

'But damn it! You didn't!' Leaving her side Andrew strode across the room. By the door there was light from the street lamp below, but he stood in the shadows. 'You did it for me and, in return, I seduced you, robbed you of your virtue...you were right when you said that having an affair would be tawdry.' The disembodied words sprang from the darkness. 'I feel as if I'd blasphemed.'

'Since I'm an ordinary mortal who's much less than perfect, your conscience can rest easy,' Elizabeth said.

'Not until you marry me.'

'Are you saying that you love me?'

'I'm saying that I want to make reparation for tonight.'

'And you think that marriage will do that?' She grabbed the back of a dining-room chair to hold herself up.

'No, but it's the best that I can do.' He sighed heavily. 'I took precautions. There won't be any reminders in nine months.'

'Isn't making an honest woman out of me a little old-fashioned?' The words gave no hint of the pain that tore at her.

'I don't want you berating yourself after I'm gone, wishing that you'd saved your virginity for your husband.' A wry note entered his voice. 'At least, if you marry me, you'll have done that.'

She fumbled for words, scarcely knowing what she was saying. 'And once we're married, what then?'

'I'll be leaving town come fall. I won't fight any divorce action you want to take. I'll step out of your life as if we'd never met.'

'Suppose I don't want a divorce? Suppose I want to go with you?'

'Impossible!' he snapped. 'I've told you before that I won't expose a woman to my life. It's too lonely, too hard. I considered it once. I won't make the same mistake twice.'

'I see. I assume that that means we won't be sleeping together any more.'

He moved swiftly to grab her shoulders. 'The hell we won't.' He thrust his hands into her hair and held her face immobile. 'Dammit, I wanted you the first time I saw you. You were drenching me with the hose and all I could think about was how much I wanted to rip that wet T-shirt off your body and take into my mouth one of those hard nipples that were pointed so arrogantly at me.'

Despite the anger in his voice, a thrill of desire coursed through her veins at his words. 'I wanted you, too,' she said.

'Of course you did—I made sure of that. And now you're in my blood. Like a disease. I want you here where I can get my fill of you. Maybe once that happens, when I leave I can forget all about you.' His mouth covered hers in a deep kiss of possession.

She yielded, but when he took impatient hold of the shirt she was wearing and attempted to remove it she shook off his hands. 'What happened to it being solely my decision? No regrets or recriminations, you said. No commitments.'

'Dammit, why didn't you listen to everything I said? I warned you how single-minded I am, but you wouldn't stay away.' He sighed heavily. 'We'll get married as soon as we can. Linda, at least, will be elated.'

'Forget it. I have no intention of marrying you.'

He was behind her going into the bedroom. 'Why not?'

'I don't want to.' She grabbed up her clothes and went into the bathroom.

He followed her. 'If it's a question of money, I'll be generous in a settlement.'

'Don't be offensive.' Obviously he had no intention of leaving her alone to dress. She turned her back to him, dropped his shirt on the floor and reached for her underwear.

Andrew picked up his shirt and tossed it in the hamper. 'You have to let me try and make things right for you.'

Elizabeth tugged her jeans into place and thrust her arms into her blouse before facing him. 'If your conscience is bothering you, that's your problem. I have absolutely no desire to marry a man because he thinks that he besmirched some mythical angel. When I marry, I intend to marry a man who wants a flesh and blood wife who will go through life at his side. What kind of marriage would it be when the bridegroom was filing his divorce papers even as he said his vows?'

'I told you——'

'I know. Your life is too dangerous to allow a mere woman to share it.' She stopped and jabbed her finger into his chest. 'In the first place, that's insulting, and in the second place, I wouldn't share your life if you offered me a million of your dumb old oil wells.'

He followed her back into the living-room. 'You're acting hastily, Elizabeth. You haven't thought this through.'

'I am? What about you? The man who plans every move he makes. In triplicate. Don't you think that taking a woman to bed one minute and asking her to marry you the next is a trifle impulsive? Especially when you don't love her.'

'Are you angry because I didn't lie and tell you that I loved you?'

She picked up the car keys he'd dropped earlier. 'You're in no condition to drive. I'll take your car. You can pick it up in the morning at the shopping centre.'

'Elizabeth!' He stood in the doorway shouting as she ground the gears on his car. 'You can't just leave like this. You have to marry me.'

'Forget it! I could never be happy with a man who folds his clothes after he makes love.' She roared from the garage as if a thousand furies were on her trail.

'I told you that this was a good day to be at the park.' Julia skipped ahead before Elizabeth could answer.

For Elizabeth the brilliance of the sunshine was dimmed by memories of the last time she'd strolled through this park. Andrew had been walking by her side. Entrusting her with confidences of his past. That evening she'd felt the welcome stirrings of a new friendship. A friendship that had grown over the weeks, one that she'd come to enjoy and cherish. How could she have been so stupid and naïve as to dynamite that friendship by giving in to what were, after all, only adolescent desires? Not only had she driven away Andrew, but Julia was now denied Linda's friendship.

'Look, Elizabeth!' Julia shouted.

The low, flexible beam bounced up and down as the small girl ran its length. Having overcome one obstacle, Julia teetered precariously on the next before successfully reaching its summit. If only she'd been as successful in negotiating her life, Elizabeth thought bitterly. Not that all that had happened was entirely her fault. Blast Andrew for doing everything in his power to seduce her, and then, when he'd succeeded, blaming her just because he'd been overcome by a belated sense of chivalry. How arrogant of him to assume that, just because he'd decided that he was obliged to marry her, she had to agree. And how petty of him to make Julia and Linda suffer the results of his self-righteous behaviour. He had not brought Linda back to the Asher household, an action that left no doubt in Elizabeth's mind that he was serving notice. Either Elizabeth must do things his way, or he would erase her totally from his life.

The whole situation was ludicrous. He would have laughed hysterically if the tables had been reversed and she'd told him that she didn't love him but felt obliged to marry him because of some antiquated sense of honour. She should thank her lucky stars that she and Andrew hadn't fallen in love with each other. Two people who scarcely shared an identical thought had no business becoming involved with each other. The only wonder was that it had taken her so long to realise that fact.

'No wonder Linda was so insistent that we come to this particular park.'

The sarcastic words sent her spinning around. The scowl on Andrew's face made two things quite clear: Elizabeth's appearance was as unwelcome as it was unexpected. Immediately she knew that Julia's request to visit the park had not been a casual one. Before she could voice her suspicions, Andrew's next words ignited her own temper.

'If you wanted to see me, all you had to do was call. It wasn't necessary to bring the children into it,' he said.

'How do you manage to walk down the street without tripping over your own ego? I couldn't care less if I never saw you again. Anyone else would immediately realise that Linda plotted this with Julia. Living with a father like you must drive a child to all kinds of extreme measures.' She walked away, her limbs trembling with anger.

'You must admit that it looks suspicious.' Andrew kept pace with her.

'I don't admit to any such thing.' She turned and glared at him. 'But then, my mind has never worked like yours. Anyone who comes up with the crackpot ideas that you——'

'Elizabeth, quick!' Julia grabbed her hand, breathless from running. 'A kitten . . . some boys are throwing it . . . the pond . . . it'll drown!'

Before Julia had finished her explanation, Elizabeth was speeding down the path towards the pond. Andrew pounded past her. From around a curve came the sound of coarse laughter accompanied by the quacking of outraged mallards and Linda's shrill voice. The small girl cried out with gladness as Andrew sped around the corner, Elizabeth at his heels. Several boys immediately scattered. Before Elizabeth could reach the green, brackish water, Andrew had plunged down the rocky steps into the pond. Elizabeth grabbed Linda from her precarious perch on a wobbly rock and, following the direction of the child's finger, spotted the object of Andrew's mission. At the same moment, Andrew thrust his hand into the water and came up with a bedraggled mass of fur. Splashing to the side of the pond, he sat down on the steps and laid the soggy kitten over his knee. Heedless of his dripping trousers, he pressed gently on the kitten's back. The only response was a loud sob from Linda.

Julia came panting up. 'Is it OK?'

Elizabeth dropped to her knees and hugged both girls to her. 'I don't know.'

Andrew pressed again and again. Just when they had all given up hope, a stream of water spewed forth from the kitten's mouth and it coughed weakly. Andrew worked over the kitten for a few more minutes until they all heard the piteous miaow from the small animal. Elizabeth pulled a paper tissue from her pocket. 'This is all I have.'

Andrew dismissed her offering with a glance and pulled off his shirt. Drying the shivering animal as best he could, he wrapped it in the shirt. 'We'd better get him to a vet.'

The girls had to run to keep up with him and even Elizabeth was forced to take an occasional running step. There was no suggestion that Elizabeth and Julia remain behind.

At the veterinarian's office, the kitten was quickly whisked into an examination room. Andrew helped Linda hold the small animal while the vet deftly dealt with it. The girls needed as much consoling as the kitten when a needle was produced.

'It's for his own good,' Andrew said.

'Her own good.' The vet smiled at him. 'It appears to me that you and your wife have just added a third daughter to the family,' she said.

'We're not married,' he said. 'The girls were playing together at the park.'

'I see, Mr . . .?' She raised a questioning eyebrow.

Elizabeth could almost see the woman appraising Andrew's muscled shoulders as he told her his name. Not that Elizabeth could blame her. Her own fingers itched to spread themselves over Andrew's bare skin.

The vet smiled again. 'Do call if you have any questions. I can always be reached through my answering service. Day or night.'

'Day or night,' Elizabeth mimicked as Andrew drove her and Julia back to their car.

'Jealous?'

'Don't be absurd. I know how attracted you are to ministering angels. I simply don't think that her behaviour was very professional.'

'Don't be a dog in the manger. I offered to marry you,' he pointed out.

'An offer that appealed to me no more than it obviously appealed to Linda's mother.' The minute the words left her mouth, Elizabeth was appalled. How cruel of her to throw salt in old wounds. Just because for one moment when she'd heard his voice in the park she'd thought that he'd arranged their meeting. Just because he'd acted without hesitation when he'd been needed. Just because the sight of his bare chest melted her insides. Just because the thought of the veterinarian's pretty face resting against that chest in Andrew's bed caused her unbearable pain.

The silence in the car hung heavily over her and she endeavoured to turn Andrew's thoughts in another direction. 'What will you do with the kitten?' She looked over her shoulder. The two girls were intent on the cat.

'Call the Humane Society and see if anyone reported her missing. Put an ad in the paper.' He glanced in the rear-view mirror.

'My guess is that she was abandoned,' Elizabeth said. 'How will you ever persuade Linda to give her up? I'm afraid she's already thinking up names for her.'

Andrew gave her a mocking glance. 'What makes you think that you're the only angel of mercy around? Is it so hard to believe that I would allow Linda to keep her kitten?'

'But what would you do with it when Linda leaves?'

They were back at the car park. 'Send it with her,' he said.

'Of course, how silly of me. At the end of the summer you intend to get rid of all encumbrances. Mail your daughter and her pet back east. Divorce your wife.' She stepped from the car. 'It's just like paper plates. Use them for the summer and then toss them away.' The loud slam of the car door echoed behind her.

Elizabeth drove herself and Julia home through a veil of tears. Andrew hadn't even bothered to deny her accusation. But then, how could he defend himself from the truth?

Truth. A commodity that had been in short supply lately. If she'd told Andrew the truth about their initial encounter, he never would have seduced her. That was one truth. The other was one that she'd been avoiding admitting, even to herself.

She pounded the steering wheel with her fist. How had she ever allowed herself to get so entangled with him? She had thought she was so clever. Appointing herself an authority on how he should live his life. She'd even laughed about how she was creating a new Andrew. It had become a game with her. A game that she'd lost. Because the creator had fallen in love with her creation.

Except that that wasn't entirely true. She hadn't created a new Andrew or even a better one. Andrew's good qualities had been there all along. She had simply been blind to them. So intent on demonstrating to him that life had its less serious side, she'd taken scant notice of virtues like dependability, honesty, courage, thoroughness, tenacity... So what if he didn't laugh a hundred times a day? Andrew had reacted to the kitten's predicament without a thought for his own comfort or safety, and he'd ruined an expensive shirt without hesitation. Maybe Andrew did arrange his life with military precision, but he'd proved that he could easily shed his plans when necessary. And how could she have ignored the way that he'd disrupted his entire life for his daughter? Andrew was as solid as a rock, a man a woman could lean on and depend upon.

Not any woman. Elizabeth Asher. She wanted him. Ballast that would keep her life on course. The problem was, he didn't want her. She dashed away tears with an impatient hand. She was fine for sharing his bed, but he'd made it quite clear that a woman, especially a frivolous woman like her, one tied to her family, had no place in his life. In his eyes she was an object of desire, not a helpmate who could slog through the hard times of life with him.

And what about her family? Even if Andrew did love her, following him around the globe meant abandoning her family. They needed her as much as Andrew did. The only difference was, they knew it. For a moment she allowed herself to contemplate acceptance. Andrew, hers for the moment, and she wouldn't even have to leave her family. She shook her head. Andrew's way would be committing emotional suicide. Loving him as she did, how could she ever let him leave her once the summer was gone? By then he would have become such a part of her that ripping him from her life would be as painful as ripping off an arm or a leg. She couldn't trade a few weeks of paradise for a lifetime of hell. And even paradise would be tainted because, no matter how well Andrew loved her in the bedroom, she would always know that such love was merely desire and in the end he'd walk away without a backward glance.

Back at home, Julia raced into the house ahead of her.

Elizabeth was hanging the car keys on the hook when her mother walked into the kitchen. 'Julia said that there was something wrong,' Anna Belle said. She took one look at the tears streaming down her oldest daughter's face and pressed her down on the nearest chair. 'Tell me,' she demanded.

Elizabeth sobbed out the entire story.

'He does love you,' her mother said. 'He's simply afraid to admit it.'

Elizabeth shook her head. 'It's hopeless.'

Anna Belle squeezed her hand. 'A hopeless problem simply takes a little longer. With all of us putting our heads together, we'll solve it. You'll see.'

CHAPTER NINE

ELIZABETH looked at her watch. Chan and Tommy should be arriving with him any time now. She hoped that there hadn't been any trouble. They'd disapproved of the idea from the beginning. It had taken tears to convince them. Tears and the surprising combined support of Max, Anna Belle, Paige and Mrs Clairmont. She giggled at the memory. Only the threat of Anna Belle sending the whole family had kept Max from participating in the kidnapping. Anna Belle was probably in her studio right now working on Elizabeth's wedding dress.

And Mrs Clairmont. Elizabeth's inspired idea. If it weren't for Mrs Clairmont, Elizabeth might not be sitting out on the prairie in a ramshackle, abandoned cabin at this very minute. Because Mrs Clairmont, when approached by Elizabeth and Max with the proposition, had not only broken down and cried: she'd said yes, and acted with such promptitude that they'd begun moving her things that very day, and her house was already cleaned and available for rent.

Renting was Max's idea. In case things didn't work out. But it was already evident that things were going to work out very well. Mrs Clairmont, who'd quickly been dubbed Clary, took no more notice of mess or noise than she did of dogs and cats underfoot. Even her beloved dachshund had quickly made friends with the other animals. And while everyone claimed that they could not possibly manage without Elizabeth, she noticed that they never said that when they were eating Clary's delicious cooking. Clary had already baked the wedding cake. It was sitting in the freezer waiting to be iced. Waiting for the groom.

Who was—where? Elizabeth looked impatiently at her watch once more. Only five minutes had crawled by. Would he be furious? Kidnapping would be an awful affront to his dignity. His parents were to call his office and take care of Linda. They'd hardly been surprised when Elizabeth had contacted them and told them her plans. It seemed that Linda had been recruited as a spy after all—by her grandmother. Elizabeth had decided not to wait until the child had returned to her mother because she knew that Linda wouldn't want to miss the wedding.

The wedding. Her wedding. She repeated the words over and over again as if they were a magical incantation that would make her dreams a reality. As Anna Belle had promised, the hopeless only took a little longer to solve. Not that this problem was by any means solved. Clary's taking over the household reins had solved only a minor part of her problem, which was humorous when she thought about it. All these years she'd felt that she could never leave her family to manage without her. Funny how easy that was turning out to be, now that she had fallen in love with Andrew.

Standing at the window, she glanced at her wrist. Was the whole world moving in slow motion today? Outside, a tall plume of dust caught her eye. A car on the dirt road. The column spiralled nearer. It was them. Him. Her stomach took a sudden, queasy dip. The whole idea was absolutely insane. What had they been thinking of? Even if he didn't hate her forever, suppose he brought charges? How could she have involved Chan and Tommy?

She ran from the window. The wood was warped by weather and age and the door opened with a piercing shriek. Tommy and Chan, looking slightly dishevelled, were helping Andrew from the back seat of Chan's car. A blue bandana tied around Andrew's head covered his eyes.

'Where am I?' Andrew demanded.

'Shut up and walk,' Tommy growled in a barely disguised voice.

Elizabeth conquered a grin. Tommy had apparently got thoroughly into his character. Chan looked slightly harassed as he guided Andrew up the one step, giving a terse direction with a falsetto voice.

'On the bed,' Elizabeth directed. 'Do you have the handcuffs?' There was no point in disguising her voice. Andrew would find out soon enough.

'Elizabeth?' Andrew asked incredulously.

She ignored him for a moment. 'He's right-handed. Fasten that hand. Leave the other free. Be careful of his shoulder.' Her brothers worked silently and then Elizabeth followed them from the house. A few murmured instructions, and they drove away. She went back inside. Andrew had removed his blindfold.

'Care to explain?' he asked.

His calm question didn't deceive her. He was seething. 'I have several explanations ready. Which would you like?'

'The truth,' he bit out.

Elizabeth smiled, a slow one designed to aggravate him. She noticed that it worked. 'It could be that I had you kidnapped to be my love slave.' She sat down out of his reach. 'You see, when you made love to me you aroused me to such heights of passion that I knew that I had to have you in my bed until you'd burned out the fires of desire.' She was wearing her tight jeans and a gingham blouse. Slowly she unbuttoned the blouse and tossed it on the bed. Near Andrew. She hoped that she'd doused it with enough perfume so that he could smell it. Beneath the blouse she'd worn only a white-knit camisole of Laura's. Designed for a less developed body, the fabric was stretched to its sheerest limits and Elizabeth was well aware that the tips of her breasts were dark shadows beneath the knit. If she hadn't known, the look on Andrew's face would have told her.

'If I'm to be your love slave, don't you think you ought to come closer?' His voice was hoarse.

Elizabeth shook her head. 'I said that that *could* be why I had you kidnapped. Surely an intelligent man like you would spot the flaw in that plan immediately.'

'Would I?' He was wary now, sensing the trap.

Elizabeth hoped that her smile was as patronising as she intended. 'Only a fool would think that making love to a woman would cure him of his desire for her. It hardly compares to eating chocolate until you're sick of it,' she added in a kindly voice.

'So now I'm a fool, am I?'

'Why, Andrew, I didn't say that.'

'You don't have to draw me a picture,' he said. 'This is all revenge because I dared to question the staying power of your charms.'

Elizabeth stood up and walked to the door.

'Where are you going?'

'Outside. I have no intention of sitting here and listening to your verbal abuse,' she replied.

'OK, I'm sorry. Get back here.'

Elizabeth sat down. 'You have to remember that I'm the one who's calling the shots.'

'When I get free we'll see who's calling the shots.'

Elizabeth shook her head. 'Threatening me isn't a good idea.' She stood up again.

'All right. I'm sorry. Stay here.'

She gave him an expectant look.

'Please,' he added in a grudging voice.

Elizabeth smiled. Really, this was getting to be quite entertaining, but she'd better call a halt to her teasing. Andrew would never forgive her if she made him grovel. 'This cabin is out in the middle of nowhere. No one has lived here for years.' She looked around. Cobwebs decorated the high corners of the single-room building, a window was missing a pane of glass and the newspapers that had been glued to the walls in the distant past were yellowed and peeling. She'd pounded the loose nails back into the floor, but the wooden boards were still warped and uneven with large gaps between them. 'The pump at the sink delivers only cold water. And that erratically. There's no electricity, no phone, no television, no radio and no transportation back to town. I guess we're stuck here.'

'Until?'

'Until . . . who knows?'

'And in the meantime?'

'You can co-operate or you can spend the entire time chained to the bed,' she said.

'What does co-operation entail?'

'Not trying to get away. Staying inside the cabin or with me at all times.'

'And if I refuse?'

Elizabeth shrugged. 'You might get awfully uncomfortable. I don't think the handcuffs will allow you to reach the outhouse. Of course, there is a chamber-pot under the bed.'

Andrew's eyes narrowed thoughtfully. 'And, once I'm loose, what's to prevent me from leaving?'

'Your word.'

'I see.' He studied her face. 'What's to prevent me from tossing you on the bed and ripping off your jeans?'

Elizabeth could feel the hot colour climbing up her neck. 'I told you. All I'm asking is that you not try to leave.'

He gave a short nod with his head. 'All right. I promise. Turn me loose.'

She pulled the key from her pocket and leaned over and unsnapped the cuffs. Before she could straighten up she was flat on her back on the bed, Andrew looming over her. He hadn't been given a chance to shave and his bristles scratched her skin as he pressed her deep into the mattress, using his mouth, his hands, his body to express his mastery over her. If he expected her to fight him, he was wrong. She kneaded the muscles of his shoulders as she answered his fierce kisses. When he pulled the camisole down to her waist she arched her back to bring her aching breasts nearer to his searching lips. Bolts of desire shot first from one breast and then from the other straight to the centre of her being. Elizabeth moaned.

Andrew sat up and roughly pushed her top back in place. 'I didn't get breakfast this morning. What are you cooking?'

Elizabeth almost screamed that he could make it himself, but that would have ruined her plans at the beginning. 'Bacon and eggs,' she said, lifting herself from the bed. Her calm voice denied aching flesh and a pounding heart.

A small quirk in a corner of Andrew's mouth acknowledged her tiny victory. He stood in the open doorway. 'Where are we?'

'Nowhere.' She knew what Andrew was seeing. The land was some that Max had purchased for developmental purposes. Miles and miles of prairie. A pair of horned larks flitting among the wild flowers was the only sign of life. Fortunately, the little hollow that sheltered the cabin also hid Pikes Peak and the Front Range from view. Chan had been instructed to drive aimlessly for three hours over as much mountainous terrain as he could. Andrew could be anywhere in Colorado, as far as he knew.

'You're pretty good with that wood-stove,' Andrew commented.

'Our family camps out a lot. I can cook on just about anything and just about anywhere.'

Breakfast was delicious. It should have been. Elizabeth had come out the previous day and practised for hours until she'd learned the secrets of the cantankerous stove. Andrew was obviously ravenous and he spoke only to ask for something.

He sat back in his chair. 'Now what?'

'Now I clean.' Earlier she had pumped water into a pot and set it on the stove to heat. Now she poured some of the water into a large tub and dumped the dishes in it. The dishes washed and dried, she swept the cabin. The cobwebs were next and then she polished the windows until they shined. Andrew sat in the old rocking-chair and watched her. He never said a word until he asked about lunch.

Elizabeth wiped her hand across her brow and took off the bandana that covered her hair. 'Sandwiches,' she said, and set about making them. Lunch was as silent as breakfast. The afternoon was a repeat of the

morning, with Elizabeth working and Andrew rocking
and watching her. At last the cabin was as clean as
she could make it.

Next came the bed. She glanced at Andrew doubt-
fully. No, she'd better do it herself. The mattress was
as lumpy as it was heavy. How they'd ever manage
to sleep on it... Lugging it outside, she propped it
against the house and beat it with a broom. Dust flew
up her nose and started her sneezing. Andrew lounged
in the doorway watching her. He only moved to get
out of her way as she struggled back into the cabin
with her ungainly burden. At least the sheets were
from home, fresh and sweet-smelling. And the one
blanket. Max had suggested more, at which Anna
Belle and Elizabeth had looked at each other and
laughed. The plan had seemed so simple then. Now
she wondered, but she was committed. If she didn't
carry through and Andrew moved on without her...

Andrew. Whatever his present thoughts were, he
was keeping them to himself. There had been no re-
currence of the incident earlier on the bed. And what
had that been all about? She'd die before asking him.
If only he'd say something. 'I'm going to pick some
wild flowers. You can move the rocker to the porch.'
She couldn't allow him to walk too far from the cabin.

Her overture was met with silence and she trounced
from the cabin. Stubborn man. On the wings of that
thought came the realisation that expecting him to be
happy about being kidnapped was a little too much
to ask of any man. As she stooped to pick a stalk of
orange Indian paintbrush, she noticed that he'd moved
to lounge on the steps of the old porch. Deliberately
she turned her back to him. She was wearing her
tightest jeans and she could almost feel his eyes
burning holes in the worn denim. At least he was still

interested. From nearby came the trilling of a meadow-
lark and Elizabeth hummed along with the melodic-
sounding bird as she collected more paintbrush, yellow
sunflowers, lavender vetch, white prickly poppies and
sweet clover, until she held a large bouquet.

Back at the cabin the wild flowers perfumed the air
with their heavy scent. Soup had been bubbling on
the stove-top all afternoon, and now she quickly mixed
up biscuits to accompany it. A checked tablecloth
covered the table, the jar of wild flowers set in the
middle. Andrew failed to compliment her efforts but
he ate three bowls of soup, so she supposed that that
was the same thing. After dinner he returned to the
rocking-chair.

'I have some playing cards if you're interested,' she
suggested.

'No.'

Her spirits plummeted. Nothing was going as she'd
planned. Her fingers were red and sore, her back
ached, her skin itched beneath her filthy clothes and
she longed for her bath-tub. Suddenly she remembered seeing a large metal tub at the back of the cabin,
and she went looking for it. The bottom was covered
with dirt and dead insects but there didn't appear to
be any holes in it. She dragged it around to the door
and carried bucket after bucket of fresh water outside
until it was thoroughly rinsed out. For a moment she
contemplated bathing outside, but a mosquito in
search of its dinner cancelled that idea. Heating the
water on the stove, Elizabeth half filled the tub. The
cabin was only one-roomed, but she had no intention
of hanging up a blanket for privacy. She pinned up
her hair and then, turning her back to Andrew, she
dropped her clothes on the floor.

The tub was a tight squeeze even with her knees bent, but the water was refreshing and the wood-stove still gave off enough heat to warm her. Elizabeth relaxed with a loud sigh. Behind her the creaking of the rocking-chair betrayed Andrew's faster rocking. She ignored him, lathering her body heavily with soap. Her arms, her chest, her legs—one held in the air at a time. Kneeling, she cleansed her stomach and squeezed water down her back. Then she stood and poured fresh water over her body. The creaking grew louder. She dried herself off and slid her new nightie over her head. Thin straps held up the scrap of mint-green satin that barely covered an area from breasts to the top of her thighs. No pioneer woman would have worn such a garment. But then, no pioneer woman had had Anna Belle designing her clothes.

'Coming to bed?' she asked.

'Where?' He was looking out of the window into the night.

'Your choice. The other half of the bed or the floor.' She blew out the oil lamp. 'Goodnight.'

The mattress lurched beneath his weight and Elizabeth held her breath, but he didn't reach for her. She understood now that this was a battle of wills. She'd give him a few minutes. She might have underestimated his resistance, but then, he'd misjudged her determination. His breathing was even beside her when she shivered ostentatiously. 'Chilly tonight, isn't it?'

He rolled so that his back was to her. She grinned in the dark. Did he really think that that would put her off? She scooted across the bed until her back was pressed firmly against his. 'Ummm. That's better.' She squirmed around to give emphasis to her words.

'Damn you.'

She'd forgotten how quickly he could move. Not
that it mattered. Not when she'd got what she wanted:
his lips on hers. This time he didn't leave her.

Later, as they lay breathing heavily, a warm tangle
of arms and legs, she decided that the time had come
to step up her campaign. 'I love you,' she said,
pressing a soft kiss upon his heaving chest.

Only a small jerk of his body indicated that he'd
heard her. Elizabeth fell asleep, the hairs on his chest
tickling her cheek.

And at first she thought that that was what had
awakened her, but they'd shifted in their sleep and
she lay on her back with Andrew on his stomach
beside her, one arm flung heavily across her body.
She resisted the urge to caress him and contented
herself with studying the strong lines of his face. There
was strength there, and determination. She giggled
soundlessly. Between the two of them they'd produce
children as stubborn and unyielding as steel. Her body
throbbed with the satisfying aches of a woman who'd
worked hard and been loved well.

She closed her eyes. A sound from across the room
penetrated the advancing mists of sleep. Her ears
strained to locate and identify the source of the noise.
It came from near the stove. Moving cautiously,
Elizabeth slid from under Andrew's arm. He muttered something and she froze, but he slept on. On
bare feet she crept across the room, reaching out with
her hand to locate candles and matches from behind
the stove. Shielding the light from Andrew with her
body she looked around, but saw nothing amiss until
she looked down. A small mouse had fallen into the
half-filled tub and was wearily struggling for his life.
'Poor thing,' Elizabeth said softly. Grabbing the kin-
dling bucket, she dumped its contents on the floor

and used it to scoop the mouse from his watery grave. Too exhausted to move, he huddled wetly at the bottom of the bucket. In spite of her efforts, the door protested as she opened it. She laid the bucket on its side on the ground and tapped the bottom. The mouse crept fearfully into the open and then dashed for safety beneath the cabin.

Elizabeth returned to bed. Andrew was waiting for her. If she'd put in a long, arduous day, he had not. She fell asleep in his arms, her body numbed equally by exhaustion and pleasure.

'What's for breakfast?'

Elizabeth groaned and opened her eyes. Andrew was watching her, his head propped on one fist. 'I'll never move again,' she said.

'Weakling.'

The taunt galvanised her and she sat up abruptly. 'Pancakes.'

Andrew forked a bite dripping with syrup into his mouth. 'What was all that racket about last night? I thought a banshee was trying to sneak in here.'

'The door could use a little oiling,' Elizabeth admitted, before explaining about their night-time visitor.

'I thought women were supposed to shriek and stand on chairs when they see mice.'

'You think lots of dumb things about women. And you have a terrible tendency to generalise. I'd think that that would be a dangerous habit for an engineer to have.' She reached for the plate of pancakes. 'More?'

Andrew didn't refer to the mouse again until he returned from a trip outside. 'After having my hand slapped, figuratively speaking, about the mouse, I'll ask first. How do you feel about snakes?'

'Just fine. As long as they keep their distance.'

'That might present a problem.'

Elizabeth gave him a sharp look. She mistrusted the amusement in his voice. 'Why?'

'A rattlesnake seems to have taken up residence on the cement stoop of the outhouse.'

She rushed outside to check. Andrew was probably teasing her. One look at the rattler coiled on the step disabused her of that notion. Obviously the stoop retained yesterday's heat and the snake had crawled up there to get warm.

'Does that mean we can go back to Colorado Springs now?' Andrew asked.

'No. It means we use the bushes.' Elizabeth stomped back into the house. Just how much longer before she could safely spring her proposition on Andrew?

The day was a duplication of the previous one. Andrew rocked and said little while Elizabeth worked. She emptied her bath-tub, washed the dishes, swept the floor and cooked. A slight breeze was blowing so she strung a rope she'd found under the bed between the cabin and the old windmill, to the distress of a pair of nesting swallows. Ignoring the birds swooping overhead, she filled the tub outside and washed the clothes she'd worn yesterday as well as the bed sheets. Andrew sat on the steps and watched her, the only emotion on his face a quickly hidden smile when she surprised a jack-rabbit at the base of the windmill and jumped in surprise herself as the animal leaped away.

After dinner she brought in the sheets, sweet-smelling from the prairie breezes, and remade the bed before taking a bath. This time when she finished

Andrew hauled the tub outside and emptied it, before filling it for his own bath.

Elizabeth lay in the bed watching him. The oil lamp cast his shadow hugely on the walls. Enormous shoulders, long thighs, strong arms . . . she could feel her breasts swelling beneath the covers. Any fears that he might turn his back to her tonight vanished when he slid under the covers and reached for her.

No visitor disturbed her rest during the night, but morning still came all too soon. She swore that she could hear her muscles creaking as she crawled out of bed to put the kettle on to boil for instant coffee. The soft lowing of cows in a neighbouring field came in through the broken window. Andrew was awake and she could feel him watching her. She tried to hum a gay tune but her heart wasn't in it. How much longer could she keep this up? Andrew was hardly yielding. He hadn't jumped the night before when she'd told him she loved him, but he hadn't said anything either. The wild flowers had wilted and she dumped them out of the door, but their pungent fragrance remained.

Breakfast was eaten in silence. Elizabeth removed their dishes, shook the cloth and started to wipe off the old wooden table. Her thoughts elsewhere, she was careless, and she rammed a long splinter deep into her hand. With a sharp cry she dropped her rag and grabbed the injured hand with her other one.

Andrew was instantly at her side. He took one look at her hand and swore viciously before yanking the wood from her hand. Fortunately the splinter came out in one piece. Andrew squeezed painfully on her hand until blood spurted out. 'To clean it,' he said briefly. He dragged her over to the sink and held her hand under the pump. With one hand he operated the pump while the other continued to squeeze the blood from her wound.

Elizabeth bit her lip at the pain. She couldn't cry. It would be unbearable if all her plans came to nought because of a tiny splinter.

Andrew finally shut off the pump. 'First-aid kit?' he asked.

Elizabeth nodded. 'By my suitcase.'

Andrew patted her hand dry, squeezed some antiseptic on it and stuck on a small bandage. Grabbing her other hand, he placed it beside the first on the table. Both were red and cracked. He turned them over. The backs were worse. 'This has gone far enough.'

Elizabeth tried to retrieve her hands. 'They're not so bad. I meant to bring hand-lotion but I forgot.'

'I suppose rubber gloves would have ruined your plans,' he said.

She took a deep breath. It was now or never. 'Yes. I wanted to prove that I wasn't some hothouse flower who couldn't survive without modern amenities.'

'Except toilets,' he said. At her startled look, he added, 'You accepted the snake a little too complacently. I followed you this morning when you went out to answer nature's call. Right down to the farmhouse hidden behind that hill. I watched you let yourself in with the key and then I peeked in the garage and saw your car.'

'You weren't supposed to leave the cabin.'

'I wanted to know what you were up to. Chan and Tommy wouldn't tell me much the other morning. Oh, yes,' he correctly interpreted her start of surprise, 'I knew them. You didn't really think that I'd come quietly, did you? I've spent too many years in dangerous places to be easily kidnapped by a couple of uneasy amateurs. We had a long conversation and I agreed to play along if they wouldn't tell you that I knew. I didn't put on the blindfold until we were almost here.'

'That's cheating!'

'Cheating! You can talk about cheating!' He grabbed her up off the chair and dumped her on the bed, pinning her in place with his strong arms. 'You kidnap me and flaunt your naked body in front of me and then have the nerve to say that I'm cheating!'

She closed her eyes, hoping to ward off betraying tears. 'I suppose that you were laughing at me the whole time.'

'Only when you were tiptoeing across the floor with that ridiculous mouse. I couldn't imagine what you were up to.' He dropped to her side. 'Is that to be my fate for the rest of my life? Never to know what you're up to?'

Her heart skipped a beat. 'Is that what you want?'

'What do you think?' He hesitated. 'I asked you badly the last time. I'd like to try again.' He raised one of her hands to his lips. 'Will you marry me, Elizabeth Asher?'

'Will you let me follow you all over the world?'

'Whenever possible,' he promised. 'How could I bear to let you out of my sight?' A deep kiss punctuated his words. 'The first time I fell in love with you was when you held me to your breast and comforted me. I knew I never wanted you to leave me.'

'That doesn't count,' Elizabeth objected. 'You weren't even in your right mind.'

'I haven't been in my right mind since I met you.' He ducked her playful fist. 'All right. The second time I fell in love with you was when we got drowned.'

'The wet T-shirt. That doesn't count. Lusting after my body isn't love.'

He laughed. 'I don't mean the first time. The time we got caught kissing by your treacherous sprinklers.'

'But you were furious with me.'

'Until it dawned on me that every other woman of my acquaintance would have blamed me for getting her into such a predicament and been angry that I'd wrecked her hair or her make-up or some other life-shattering thing. But you just laughed.'

'I still think that it was the wet T-shirt again.'

'Maybe,' he conceded. 'But if you keep reminding me about it I'm not going to be able to finish my recitation.'

'There's more?'

'Lots. The next time I fell in love was when you delved into my child-raising methods, protecting Linda.'

'Even though she didn't need it.'

'You didn't know that. Then, the picnic. You were lying there with Hewie tucked against your tummy and, while I was envying him, I was also thinking how much I wanted to give you a child of mine to hold and to love.'

'So you propositioned me?'

He leered down at her. 'I've never made a secret of the fact that I planned to get you in my bed.'

'You and your plans,' Elizabeth said.

'Worked, didn't it?'

'I didn't notice that you were so thrilled with the results.'

'I admit to a temporary setback. Marriage just didn't seem possible for me. After our blow-up the other night I tried to convince myself that it was better that we'd ended our relationship. That day in the park——'

'When you were so unhappy to see me.'

'I was jubilant. I thought you'd arranged it. Then the look of surprise on your face when you saw me. And you weren't exactly friendly.'

'Me? You were the one who was so hostile,' Elizabeth said.

'Because I'd missed you so much. And I didn't think that you'd missed me. It wasn't until after I got home that a few things hit me. You were jealous of the vet.' He dropped a quick kiss on her open lips. 'Yes, you were. And you were angry because I refused to take a wife with me. And, gradually, I found myself seriously considering it. That's when I realised not only that I was in love with you, but that I'd misjudged you. You can take the rough with the smooth. I'd faulted you for not taking life seriously, but I failed to appreciate the fact that one thing you always take very seriously is the welfare of others, be it a stranger along the highway, abused animals or a lonely child. There's no end to the love and generosity you share with the entire world. And you have your priorities straight: laugh at the little things and save your energies for the big problems.'

He sounded as if he was reciting a list. Elizabeth sat up and looked at him in horror. 'Don't you dare tell me that you wrote down all the pros and cons of marrying me!'

'What gave you that idea?'

'Never mind. Why didn't you share all these revelations with me?'

'I was going to call you that fateful morning when I was kidnapped. I'd decided that I wasn't leaving until you left with me as my wife. My own personal guardian angel.' He reached for her. 'So I think that we can say that my plan was successful.'

Elizabeth turned her head away from his searching lips. 'I'm no angel. Besides, I haven't agreed to marry you yet,' she pointed out.

'Then do.'

'No,' she said.

'No?'

'No, I'm not going to marry you.'

'Damn you, Elizabeth, you may not live long enough to marry anybody. Why the hell are you turning me down?'

'I've thought about it and I just can't take a chance on it.'

'I warn you, Elizabeth . . .'

She scooted to the other side of the bed. 'Andrew, you can't expect me to spend the rest of my life as Mrs Andrew T. Harcourt when I don't even know what the "T" stands for.'

There was a long silence before Andrew finally spoke. "Tulip.'

At the lugubrious pronouncement, Elizabeth clapped her hand over her mouth. Too late. Andrew heard the giggle.

'Sure, go ahead—laugh. Ha, ha. Funny, funny.'

Sitting up, she pulled a pillow across her stomach. 'Why Tulip?'

'After my mother's favourite relative, Tulip Quinn. Uncle Tooly was a bachelor who'd always spoiled her and she wanted to do something nice for him. My father went along with it because Uncle Tooly was a millionaire.' He paused. 'When he died, his will left everything to charity.'

His eyes were closed and the mournful expression on his face reminded her of Barney after someone had yelled at him. She moved back to his side and ran her finger along his jaw. His heavy growth of beard rasped at her skin. 'Andrew Tulip Harcourt.' She tried it out. 'I think I like it.' She lay back down beside him. Her finger was tracing the outline of his lips. 'Andrew Tulip Harcourt.' This time she purred his name. 'Whenever you get too stuffy or get out of line, I'll call you that.'

'I suppose you think it's a weapon you can use against me to get your own way.'

'Yup.' She rubbed his leg with hers and started nibbling on his ear.

'You're right about one thing. You're no angel.' His hand trailed down her side. 'Lizzie.'

She froze. 'You wouldn't call me that?'

'I'll even write a reminder of it in my notebook. The one where I keep track of all my plans.'

'If you do...' She sat up and started removing her clothes. 'I'll be forced to do something impulsive. Like this.'

'I've always loved that about you. Your impulsiveness, I mean. I plan to take advantage of it. Daily.'

'I've always loved that about you,' she mimicked. 'Your planning, I mean.'

'Good. I hope you'll love what I'm planning to do now.'

'Demonstrate and we'll see.'

Later she had only one complaint. And it wasn't really a complaint. 'You never told me that engineers could be so innovative.'

'Contingency plans, Angel. Contingency plans.'

HARLEQUIN
Romance

**This June, travel to Turkey
with Harlequin Romance's**

**THE JEWELS OF HELEN
by Jane Donnelly**

She was a spoiled brat who liked her own way.

Eight years ago Max Torba thought Anni was self-centered—
and that she didn't care if her demands made life impossible
for those who loved her.

Now, meeting again at Max's home in Turkey, it was clear he
still held the same opinion, no matter how hard she tried to
make a good impression. "You haven't changed much, have
you?" he said. "You still don't give a damn for the trouble you
cause."

But did Max's opinion really matter? After all, Anni had no
intention of adding herself to his admiring band of female
followers....

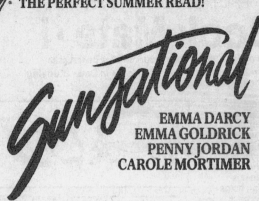

You'll flip . . . your pages won't!
Read paperbacks *hands-free* with

Book Mate • I

The perfect "mate" for all your romance paperbacks

Traveling • Vacationing • At Work • In Bed • Studying • Cooking • Eating

Perfect size for all standard paperbacks, this wonderful invention makes reading a pure pleasure! Ingenious design holds paperback books OPEN and FLAT so even wind can't ruffle pages – leaves your hands free to do other things. Reinforced, wipe-clean vinyl-covered holder flexes to let you turn pages without undoing the strap . . . supports paperbacks so well, they have the strength of hardcovers!

Pages turn WITHOUT opening the strap

SEE-THROUGH STRAP

Reinforced back stays flat

Built in bookmark

BOOK MARK

BACK COVER HOLDING STRIP

10 x 7¼ opened
Snaps closed for easy carrying, too